GOLDA SLEPT HERE

SUAD AMIRY is the founder and director of the Riwaq Center for Architectural Conservation in Ramallah. After growing up between Amman, Damascus, Beirut and Cairo, she went on to study architecture in Beirut, Michigan and Edinburgh. Since then she has lived in Ramallah.

Also by the author:

Nothing to Lose But Your Life
Sharon and my Mother-in-Law

GOLDA SLEPT HERE

SUAD AMIRY

دار جـامـعـة حـمـد بـن خـلـيـفـة للنشر
HAMAD BIN KHALIFA UNIVERSITY PRESS

This edition was first published in English in 2014
by Bloomsbury Qatar Foundation Publishing

Second edition in 2016 by
Hamad bin Khalifa University Press
PO Box 5825
Doha, Qatar

www.books.hbkupress.com

ISBN: PB: 978-9927101465
eBook: 978-9927101441

2 4 6 8 10 9 7 5 3

Typeset by Hewer Text UK Ltd, Edinburgh
Printed and bound in Great Britain by
CPI Group (UK) Ltd, Croydon CR0 4YY

To find out more about our authors and books visit
www.books.hbkupress.com
Here you will find extracts, author interviews, details of forthcoming events
and the option to sign up for our newsletters.

CONTENTS

Part One

Suad: Remembering and Forgetting

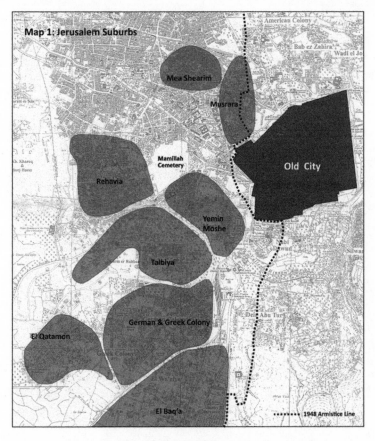

From *Jerusalem 1948: The Arab Neighborhoods and Their Fate in the War*, Salim Tamari, Editor

1.

They Missed Mama's Cooking

November 2011

E XHAUSTED, I LIE ON my back in bed, waiting for my adrenaline levels to drop.

The night promises to be long, very long.

With eyes wide open I gaze at the beautiful cross-vaulted ceiling of my bedroom at Rema and Alex's house. For the last twenty-some years they have lived in the gorgeous Hindiyeh family house in Sheikh Jarrah, an East Jerusalem Arab neighbourhood recently targeted by Jewish settlers.

I would like to think that both Rema and Alex are delighted to have a close friend descend on them from the other side of the Separation Wall. I cannot claim that I have been fun company this evening, as the acrobatics of 'illegally' sneaking into Jerusalem with Huda's help has totally drained me. Not to mention the conflicting emotions that swell my veins and the confused, and confusing, thoughts that jam my skull.

My emotions feel like a ball of entangled threads.

My head like a pressure cooker.

Though excited to see Rema and Alex, I am not in the mood to sit and chat with them all night long, as we have often done. I am extremely nervous at the mere thought of writing this book, which has been simmering within me for years now, since May 2008.

The idea for the book came to me the day my friends Mona Halabi, Huda al-Imam and other Jerusalemite women organised the Nakba Survivors Silent March commemorating sixty years of Al Nakba, The Catastrophe, the displacement and disposition of ninety percent of the Arab population in pre-Israel Palestine.

Accompanying ten Palestinian owners to their gorgeous houses and splendid villas and mansions, the one hundred or so participants in the Silent March snaked through the streets of Talbiyah, one of the most elegant Arab neighbourhoods that had become, like many other Arab neighbourhoods in West Jerusalem, exclusively Jewish.

It has taken a good three years for me to process the painful emotions and the flood of tears of the Palestinian owners as they froze and melted in front of their villas and lush gardens. It has taken me as long to come to terms with the unsettling and fearful eyes of the Israeli residents as they cautiously and nervously watched us from behind curtains and the big and small windows of those same houses.

The intolerable pain of one and the fear of the other have haunted me ever since, and pleaded with me to become the topic of my book.

So here I finally find myself venturing into Arab East Jerusalem in order to meet up with my beloved friends: Huda al-Imam and her eldest cousin, Nahil, and my neighbour Dr Gabi Baramki, the president of the university where I teach and the eldest son of the prominent Andoni Baramki, the first Palestinian architect.

Here I am, about to accompany the protagonists of my future book to their lost homes in West Jerusalem. I am full

4

of apprehension. I am dreading the terrifying act of coming face to face with their homes and the Israelis who are now residing in them. I am not sure I can bear their pain or mine. For I, so far, have never had the emotional courage to visit my own family's house in Jaffa. I saw how devastated my father was in 1968, when the Israeli family living in his house slammed the door in his face as he announced himself and asked their permission to enter his own house. I, unlike Huda, had protected my sanity all these years by avoiding going there.

Our losses were similar and so were our pains; each and every one of us dealt with them differently. While Huda dealt with her losses and pains by facing them head on, Andoni, the architect, sought justice in Israel's 'legal' system. I pretend to run away from them, or more accurately I hide behind my protagonists and their stories. I deliberately choose protagonists who deal with their losses differently.

The responsibility – or more accurately the irresponsibility – of writing a book about my friends' personal stories, their personal losses and their personal traumas terrifies me.

What concerns me most is how I have become obsessed with their obsessions, which have become my companion.

Though excited to see me, Rema and Alex also have committed a 'criminal offence' by giving me, a Palestinian without a permit, a bed (actually a mattress on the floor) in their lovely house.

Not that I had contemplated going to a hotel – none of the hotels in Arab Jerusalem would risk giving me a room – but I only hoped that the pleasure of seeing me was worth the risk that Rema and Alex were taking in hosting me for the night.

I roll on my right side trying hard to fall asleep.

5

My mother's deep voice reaches my ears. I can't help but follow it to the house just down the road from where I am lying. '*Susu habibti*, it's true that you were born in Damascus, but you were conceived in Jerusalem.' My mother smiled as she revealed this endearing detail of my conception. I was thirty years old when she surprised me with this fact. By then I had left Amman, where she and I had been living, and gone to live in Palestine. I must say having been conceived in Jerusalem was news to me – big and delightful news indeed.

'Every full moon, your Baba and I would drive from Amman to the Dead Sea, spend one night at the Lido Hotel and then drive back to Jerusalem the following day. We spent the mornings strolling in the narrow streets of Jerusalem, had a *mtabaq* at Zalatimo's, then spent the rest of the afternoon on the terrace of the National Hotel where we would stay the night, or drive to the Grand Hotel in Ramallah,' my mother said.

Though we are not meant to imagine or visualise the act of love-making that brought us into this world, that night I did. I imagined that it was an intimate and heated act. What I loved most about it was the likelihood that it followed the ecstasy of eating a yummy *mtabaq* cheese pie from Zalatimo's, my favourite sweet shop in the Old City of Jerusalem.

Since my brother Ayman and I were born a few years after the 1948 Nakba Catastrophe, I somehow felt that my mother had invented this maculate Jerusalem conception story.

To have been conceived in Jerusalem meant only one thing: my parents made love only once that weekend, otherwise how could my mother be sure that I was conceived in Jerusalem? Why not at the Dead Sea, or even Ramallah? As lovely as it sounds, I had my suspicions. Realising how happy

6

this would make me, my mother, like the Israelis (with a big difference in scale and purpose), had a tendency and talent to invent 'facts'.

I roll onto my left side, trying hard to sleep.

'Conceived on a full moon night,' Mama told me, and in this she was probably right. As my parents continued to make such trips, I personally witnessed some of these full moon nights on the Dead Sea shore. But 'conceived in Jerusalem', I'm not so sure.

One thing I do know for sure is that the house in which my newly-wed parents lived in 1942 and from which they fled in 1948 is just down the road from where I am tossing in bed in November 2011.

I also know that the two-storey house in which they had lived belonged to the Ghosheh family. The owners lived upstairs while my parents lived on the first floor. 'I loved living in Jerusalem more than any other city, simply because the Jerusalemites were aloof and stingy,' my mother always said. 'And as a result, they left you in peace. Unlike Damascus, Beirut and Salt (in Jordan) where people invite you to visit and keep you under surveillance day and night, the Jerusalemites couldn't be bothered, and hence never interfered in anyone's business.' Another virtue of my mother's, in addition to fabricating facts, was that she never praised someone without also pointing out his or her bad points. She applied the French *jolie-laide* to everything in her life, including the Jerusalemites whom she adored. 'I loved all my neighbours in Jerusalem, especially Umm Samir Ghosheh who I bartered with. I would bring her and her three daughters red lipstick and other make-up from Souq al-Hamidiyeh in Damascus. In return she prepared for me platters of stuffed

7

squash, stuffed grape leaves, stuffed potatoes, stuffed tomatoes, stuffed onions, stuffed peppers and stuffed cabbage. Of all the varieties of stuffed vegetables the ones I liked best were the stuffed purple carrots. They were so tough to core that Umm Samir had to send them to a carpenter in the Old City to drill holes in them.'

Spending so much time stuffing everything that lent itself to filling in any way or form, I am not surprised that the Jerusalemites never had the time to raise their heads or look out of their windows to see what their neighbours were up to.

Having a rich Syrian uncle, Jamil Far'oun, who owned a lovely house in the Talbiyah neighbourhood and many businesses including Taxi Abdo, a Jerusalem to Damascus taxi company, provided my mother with the edge she needed in her barter relationship with Umm Samir. With so many red lipsticks coming all the way from Damascus, my mother over-stuffed her husband and her two little daughters until they could bear no more.

Since I lacked the emotional resilience needed to visit my father's house in his hometown of Jaffa, the very first place I paid homage to when I came to Palestine in 1981 was my parents' house in Jerusalem.

'Ah! You must be Siham's daughter, Siham Jabri-al-Amiry? Oh, my God! You look so much like her!' Salma, one of the late Umm Samir's three daughters, screamed her greeting at me when I appeared at my parents' huge terrace thirty-three years after they had left it. I wanted to see the terrace on which both my sisters, Arwa and Anan, had spent their Jerusalem childhoods. Where my three-year-old sister Anan, shaking, had screamed, 'Aaaaah, take the sheep away from

8

me! Take that sheep away from me! Poor thing, poor sheep, he is so scared of me!' when my Baba brought her first 'temporary' pet to the huge terrace and large garden below it.

Looking at Salma's pale and worn face I realised the significance of the lipstick-for-food-programme initiated by my flamboyant Damascene mother for the benefit of the provincial looks and tired faces of Jerusalemite women.

Unable to sleep, I roll onto my right side again.

I then reach for the transistor radio I have placed under my pillow. Soon I am lost in an ocean of Hebrew. Some stations are coming through crystal clear, including Kol Israel and Kol Yerushalayim, while the Arabic stations are hissing. I can't help recall some of the stories that Baba had told us over the years about the Palestine Broadcasting Service (PBS) and its very first radio station, Huna al Quds (Jerusalem Calling). The PBS was a British Mandate state-owned radio station where he worked in the early 1940s until it was taken over by the Zionist forces in 1948.

Baba told sad and funny stories whenever our family sat for dinner around that long dining table in our house in Amman. I smile in bed as I remember how his strict eating habits were similar to Umm Salim's, my late mother-in-law. Not only did Baba keep a rigid British Mandate schedule for the three meals – eight, two and eight – he also imposed conversation rules. In addition to him and Mama, each one of us four children had to tell a joke or summarise what he or she had learnt that day.

While Mama's stories focused on the glory of her Damascene family, particularly her rich and good-looking father, Baba's often had a historical, political or nationalist twist to them. In spite of the many personal and national losses he suffered

9

– lost homes, a lost city, a dispersed family, a lost and shattered homeland and broadcasting station – he, like most of the Nakba generation, shied away from talking about his personal pain and immersed himself in starting a new life, with a new job, a new house, and a new everything in Diaspora.

Perhaps the wound was still open.

It wasn't until much later in my life that I realised:

The Palestinians try hard to forget when they should remember.

The Israelis try hard to remember when they should forget.

The Palestinians refuse to be victims.

The Israelis make sure that they remain the only victims.

My childhood memories oscillate between Mama's omnipresent family mansion in the splendour of the old city of Damascus, and Baba's lost house in the Manshiyeh neighbourhood of the seaside town of Jaffa. I have had to construct this house from tales and imagine it from far, far away.

But I must say, despite his great losses and seriousness, Baba had a keen sense of humour and appreciated a good story.

It was around our dining table that I had to figure out what a joke was. While my brother Ayman, two years older than me, told truly funny stories and hilarious jokes, I, the baby of the family, told the same joke over and over, every time we sat around the table. And since every single member of my family began rolling about with laughter the minute I opened my mouth, I concluded that a joke gets better and funnier the more often it is told. Perhaps there is a clue here to my adult style of talking and writing.

Unable to sleep, I turn over in bed.

I surf through more Hebrew wavelengths and think again

about Baba's lost station. From his hometown, Jaffa, he had gone to study biology at the American University of Beirut in 1924. Eager to serve his wounded country he returned home at the age of twenty-one. He helped establish a chapter of the Arab Students Club along with other nationalist activists, but soon took refuge in Jordan in order to avoid an arrest order issued by British Mandate authorities in Palestine on the eve of the 1929 Buraq uprising, the Arab revolt against the British policies favouring the migration of European Jews to Palestine.

After spending more than ten years as the director of the only senior school in the Jordanian town of Salt, Baba was delighted to accept a position as the head of the Arabic Programme at the Palestine Broadcasting Service in 1942, also known as the Palestine Broadcasting Corporation, or PBC.

On 30 March 1936 the Palestine Broadcasting Service was inaugurated with programmes running in three languages, Arabic, Hebrew and English, and airtime allocated in that order.

'Not having the letter "p" in Arabic, most Arabs pronounced it as "b". So there was tremendous confusion between the PBC and the BBC. But this was not the first time the British had taken credit both for things they do, and things they do not do.' I can still hear Baba's chuckles and see his sparkling dark eyes as he told the story around that dining table.

While Mama was busy raising her two little daughters and improving her barter programme with her Jerusalem neighbours, Baba was in constant negotiation with the British Mandate authorities to gain better terms and longer airtime for his Arabic programmes on PBS.

With tension rising and fighting escalating between Arab and Jewish forces in Jerusalem, Mama felt the need to enrol in a first aid course. Realising that his biology degree got him nowhere in the increasingly lawless jungle called Palestine, Baba, like Mama, opted for further education and began working towards a law degree at the Arab College in Jerusalem.

Meanwhile, in view of their biased policies favouring the Zionists, the British officers kept all Arabic programmes on PBS under heavy scrutiny and tight censorship. This inevitably resulted in the resignation of many Palestinians working in the Arabic section. Among those who resigned were my father's best friends: Ibrahim Tuqan, a famous Palestinian poet, and Khalil Sakakini, the eminent Palestinian educator who handed in his resignation to his British boss the minute he heard a Jewish broadcaster announce on air: 'This is Eretz Israel.' This is the Land of Israel.

'If this is Eretz Israel, then where is Ard Falastin?' yelled Khalil Sakakini at his British superior. Where is the Land of Palestine?

'Well, he says his point of view and you say yours,' explained the British officer.

'What point of view? Why does he call it Eretz Israel when the official name of this station is the Palestine Broadcasting Service?'

From what Baba reported, it seemed that both the Arabic as well as the Jewish programmes had become platforms for national awareness, debates and, of course, conflicts, and hence targets for sabotage.

On 3 August 1939, the Jewish underground militia Etzel blew up part of the radio station's offices during the children's hour. Two of its staff were killed in the bombing: a Palestinian called Adib Mansour, and a recent Jewish immigrant from South Africa named Mae Weissenberg.

In spite of the danger of it all, Mama had been delighted to

12

leave the little provincial town of Salt and come running to what turned out to be her favourite city: Jerusalem and its stuffing(s).

Nearing sleep, lying on my back with the radio pressed against my left ear wailing Hebrew songs, I can't help recall how happy Baba was when he told us a story about an Arab singer who had visited the station. Many came to perform in the live music programmes of the PBS, mostly Egyptians, but also Syrians and Lebanese.

'I was so fortunate to meet them all in person: Abdulwahab, Zakaria Ahmad, Saleh Abdulghani, Lur Dukkash, and of course Asmahan and her brother, Farid al-Atrash.' So different in appearance, it was difficult to believe that the two renowned Lebanese singers, Asmahan and Farid al-Atrash (paradoxically, *atrash* in Arabic means 'deaf'), were sister and brother. When Asmahan was killed in a car accident, there were strong rumours that the accident was orchestrated either by British intelligence, as many believed she was their agent, or by Umm Kulthum, the Maria Callas of the Arab world and Asmahan's only real competitor.

One thing I remember vividly is how much Baba and Mama wished Umm Kulthum would return to Jerusalem and to the Arabic programmes of PBS. Umm Kulthum had actually visited Jerusalem and other cities in Palestine in 1935, only a year before the inauguration of the PBS. I, like the rest of my family, was a big fan of hers, so I had memorised all the dates of her performances in Palestine by heart. The poster which my mother had framed and placed on the wall of our living room had Umm Kulthum's photo as well as the following text with dates and cities:

13

In the flourishing cities of Palestine
The great singer Umm Kulthum and her celebrated band present
the following concerts:

1, 2 May in Jerusalem (Cinema Edison)
5, 6 May in Jaffa (Theatre Opera Maghribi)
7, 8 May in Haifa (Cinema 'Ein Dour)

Much had happened in the course of the ten years that
separated Umm Kulthum's performances in the 'flourishing
cities of Palestine', and May 1948 when the British left
Palestine and all hell broke loose.

They Missed Mama's Cooking

On 4 May 1948
Having fulfilled their promise
A Jewish state over Palestine
The British packed up and went home
They claimed they missed their mothers' cooking
Roast beef and Yorkshire pudding
With boiled cabbage on the side
They simply boarded their ships and sailed away
Without a word of apology
Or farewell
The Bride was never consulted
Not in 1916 when they first landed
Nor in 1917 when Lord Balfour made his declaration
What God did not do for centuries
Lord Balfour delivered in sixty-seven words
When they arrived her name was Palestine

And when they left her name had become Israel
Being impartial rulers
Some subjects were more equal than others
They handed the new minority the majority of the land
Equity and more equity in the Empire where the sun
    never sets

15 May 1948

They left behind two fighting peoples
One strengthened, the other weakened
The new and mighty jubilated and went for more
'What is mine is mine and what is yours is also mine'
Meanwhile the old and the frail, dispossessed and
    dehumanised
Were left to mourn and lament

They mourned the larger-than-life losses. They mourned the loss of a home, of a garden, an orchard, a field, a homeland.

The loss of a sea, of mountains, hills, plains, valleys, lakes, springs, riverbeds, archaeological sites, Bedouin hamlets, villages, towns and cities.

They mourned the loss of a sun dipping in an open Mediterranean Sea.

Workers mourned the loss of their factories; professionals mourned the loss of their offices.

Merchants mourned the loss of their souqs and markets: the buzz and noise of the old town of Acre, of Haifa, Jaffa, Lod, Ramallah, Asqalan and of Asdoud.

They mourned mosques, churches, holy shrines and monasteries.

The sick missed their doctors, clinics, pharmacies and hospitals, and a few missed their mental clinics.

The fishermen mourned the loss of their sea: the uncertainty of venturing into the darkness of a treacherous sea; and their full nets at sunrise after yet another night of fishing. They missed their companions: other fishermen in small boats. They missed the big and small fish: sea bass, sardines, calamari, shrimp and the red mullet that brought them luck, and also the rare sharks of the deep sea and those of the seashore.

The peasants mourned the loss of their compact villages and vast fertile fields: the orange groves, the vineyards, the ancient olive trees, the shade of a fig tree, the flowering almond trees, the burgundy splashes of the mulberry and pomegranate trees, the thistles of the cacti.

The kids missed school but also playing in the narrow alleys, dipping their feet in the salty sea and its fine sandy beaches, riding on small donkeys and hanging down deep water cisterns.

But most of all people mourned the loss of a home. They simply missed home: they missed their fruit gardens, their living rooms, their bedrooms, their balconies, their dining rooms and tables, their formal guest room and worn-out sofas, their Persian carpets, their books and their paintings, cups and crystal glasses, kitchen cupboards full of seasonal foods and extra virgin olive oil pressed that year, shelves heavy with wedding china, closets full of old and new clothes.

They mourned the loss of a musical instrument: an oud, a drum, a hand-held daf and possibly a piano. They mourned leaving behind their photo albums and letters from a mother to her child, they missed their children's toys, teenage 78 rpm records, personal book collections. They mourned their public libraries, schools, kindergartens, football fields, hospitals, clinics, stores, cars, tractors, buses, motorcycles, bicycles, toddlers' toy cars and swings.

And when they had time to reflect on the animals they had left behind, they cried: whatever happened to the cows, horses, sheep, goats, mules, camels, donkeys, ducks and chickens, rabbits, turtles, beloved dogs and cats, and lovebirds in cages?

And who watered the thirsty horses when their owners had to run for their lives?

Ah, if only animals told their stories before they died in silence.

> As Diaspora ended for one people
> Diaspora started for another
> A new nation remembered, an old one forgotten.

Unable to sleep, I turn on my back and take a deep breath.

When the fighting between Arabs and Jews intensified in 1948, trying to spare his baby, Baba spent most of his days and nights at the PBS studios in the new broadcasting building in Talbiyah, which later became a West Jerusalem neighbourhood. Meanwhile Mama bore the heavy burden of protecting her four dear ones: her daughters Arwa and Anan, aged five and four, and their puppies Lulu and Murjan, both one year old.

And once again, with the help of her rich uncle's Taxi Abdo, Mama managed a swift trip to her family in Damascus where she left Arwa and Anan. When she hurried back she arrived to a half-occupied house and two missing puppies.

Since our home, the Ghosheh house, was strategically located it was often caught in the crossfire. Four Zionist fighters had taken refuge in our living room. Mama was assigned the task of negotiating with the occupiers, but as is often the case, what was fully and rightfully ours had already become half theirs; and like the rest of Jerusalem and Palestine, part of our house and Mama's dowry furniture fell under occupation.

As for the missing reddish-brown puppies (hence the name Murjan or 'coral'), while Umm Samir claimed enemy fighters had stolen Lulu and Murjan, others swore that the cute little puppies had been brutally slain. Hoping it was theft rather than the unspeakable, Mama's eyes filled with tears.

With the help of Ammu Adli, a family friend and a good neighbour, she loaded her share of her own dowry furniture into the back of a truck.

Off she went in the direction of Ramallah.

Like the black table around which we gathered years later, telling jokes and stories of hope and aspiration for a new and happy life in Amman, the rest of the furniture had either been grazed by bullets or pierced by direct hits: all witnesses to what Mama and Baba had been through.

'Mama, did you bring Lulu and Murjan with you?' This was the very first question that little Arwa and Anan asked as they ran to welcome their mother when she eventually rejoined them in Damascus. It was this innocent inquiry, in the safety of her family home, that finally made Mama surrender. She burst into sobs as she knelt down and hugged her two little ones.

It took my sister Anan some forty years to dig into her past and write her first short story, entitled 'Lulu and Murjan'.

Meanwhile, back in Jerusalem, Baba alongside his friend and colleague Ajaj Nuwayhid, the head of cultural programmes at PBS, and many others, carried on with the heavy responsibility of moving the broadcasting equipment from Jerusalem to Ramallah where the main transmitter was.

For the following few months, the whole family – Baba, Mama, Arwa and Anan – worked, lived and played in the corridors of the transmission building, today's Muqata'a, the Presidential Headquarters: the very same building in which the late Arafat was besieged and heavily bombarded (along with my mother-in-law) in 2003.

Ah, if only buildings could tell their stories.

'If only your Baba loved me as much as he loved his radio station and equipment!' Mama would complain over the following decades.

Whether my mother was right or, more probably, wrong about my being conceived in the Holy City, Jerusalem, you have a piece of my heart.

Yes, you have a piece of my heart.

No, not because you have been so idolised and iconised.

No, not because you've been declared the Eternal Capital in a doomed world.

No, not because of your fabricated past that has been made more important than your present.

It is because you were not allowed to be a normal city with normal people, so much so that you have become an abnormal place with abnormal people – Arabs and Jews alike.

Jerusalem, you have a piece of my heart only because you have a chunk of my mundane everyday life.

Yes, you were the very first city to welcome me back when I arrived in Palestine in the summer of 1981. I vividly recall how I hurriedly dropped my suitcase and ran out of the YMCA where I was staying, soon to be lost in your crowded souqs and narrow, labyrinthine alleys.

I slowly but cautiously had to build my relationship with you: a familiar yet very peculiar city. Mama was right: your people are certainly aloof and reserved.

It was in Jerusalem that my husband-to-be, Salim, and I had our first date: he took me to see *Lady Chatterley's Lover* (the film, that is).

Whenever I had the chance, Salim next to me, I would excitedly drive the fourteen kilometres separating the confining and provincial town of Ramallah, where we both lived (separately), from the big and open city.

I would park my little Fiat 127 in East Jerusalem to avoid having it towed away or blown up in West Jerusalem. The blue plates revealed that its owner was potential trouble. And since it was not so long ago that the Israeli army had blown up Rema's UN car, I made sure to take care of my little baby, my precious set of wheels.

We would then venture west for long strolls that took us everywhere and nowhere: to Jaffa Street, to Stiematsky's bookshop, to the Orthodox Mea She'arim Quarter for its charm and peculiarity, to the German Colony neighbourhood for a good coffee and scrumptious German pastry, to the Talbiyah neighbourhood to visit our dear friend, Judy Blanc, or to walk around admiring the architectural qualities of the Yemin Moshe. And since the Israelis had closed all the movie theatres in Ramallah and the other cities in the Occupied Territories, including East Jerusalem, and since Salim is a passionate movie-goer, we more often than not found ourselves in an Israeli cinema.

Seeking atonement for violating the boycott of enemy territory and products, we would eventually settle down to a nice meal, with terrible local wine, in one of Arab East Jerusalem's restaurants.

I must admit that the only time I felt guilt-free about not boycotting Israeli products was when it came to wine. I tipsily convinced myself that the excellent Golan Heights wines made by Israelis were kosher because they came from the occupied parts of Syria. Compared to the local Palestinian wines produced by Cremesan and Latrun, two Italian monasteries, Israeli wines were far superior. Having been away from home too long to remember how good Italian wines taste, the Italian nuns and monks had acquired local Palestinian taste (or perhaps the lack of it). Thanks to the superb made-in-Ramallah *arak*, I was able to stick, more often than not, to my boycott of Israeli goods, one of the few principles I have left.

Tipsy, Salim and I would spend the rest of the evening on the lovely terrace of the National Hotel, the same hotel where I was allegedly conceived, not so many decades earlier. Meanwhile the owners, the Abu al-Haj family, were struggling to keep it afloat in the impossible economic conditions of East Jerusalem. Sadly, it has since closed down.

Beginning to fall asleep now, my other Jerusalem connections race through my mind: Riwaq architectural projects, friends, Hakawati Theatre plays, Orient House and negotiating at 'Peace Talks', applying for visas and attending boring receptions at consulates, shopping, and finally, having to use the passport belonging to my dog, the late Nura, just to enter the city.

And look at me now, sneaking in like a thief, committing

a series of 'criminal offences' and 'illegally' crossing the many checkpoints that strangle you, Jerusalem.

I come to listen to your pain and to hear the stories and memories of a few of your obsessed citizens. Jerusalem, I come to you in disguise: in over-colourful, immodest clothes and vulgar make-up . . . The only way I could come to you was in disguise, as a whore.

Unable to sleep, I turn over and switch on the light. Come on, Suad, go easy on yourself.

It is three in the morning when I marvel at the reflection of light on an intricately spun spider's web stretched between two elaborate cast-iron window guards. Something about the spider's energy and movements make me think of Ranjani, Mama's domestic helper, who was far from home and whose house – as well as twenty-four years' worth of work – was swept away by the 2004 tsunami that hit the southern coast of her native Sri Lanka. In spite of all that, Ranjani carried on.

I think of Vanouch, my Armenian-Greek-Cypriot friend, (married to a Palestinian) whose home ended up on the other side of Nicosia, and who burst into tears when the young wife of the Turkish officer told her that the chimney in that house was a new addition. 'It was my father who built this chimney with his own hands.'

I think of Ritu, my Indian friend and publisher, who lost a home in what became Pakistan.

I think of Shams, my Pakistani friend, who misses her home in Delhi.

I think of our London-based friend, Sami Zubaida, an Iraqi Jew, who misses home: Baghdad and its Tigris.

And that makes me think of the Jewish communities who not long ago were an integral part of the former Arab world.

22

I think of the Native Americans and the Aborigines of Australia.

I must have dreamt of black Africans being dragged a long, long way from home. Like most of us, never to feel at home again.

And as I am falling asleep, I wonder why other people's pain makes me feel better.

I hear the loud beat and thrumming of drums coming all the way from Africa, only to wake up and realise that it is my friend Huda who has been banging hard on my bedroom door. I must indeed have been in deepest Africa not to have heard Huda's high-pitched voice when Rema opened the house door for her this morning.

'Suad! Suad! *Yalla, habibti*, get up. Drink your coffee. I want you fully awake. I've made you lots of appointments today, including one with PM Golda Meir. I'm going to show you the biggest real estate robbery in modern history.'

Come on, Suad, drink lots and lots of coffee.

Part Two

Andoni: A Master Builder's Passion

Andoni

'FOR YEARS MY FATHER stood in solitude across the street from his beloved. And for hours on end he stared west waiting for the sun to rise. Only death could separate them. And it did.'

There was hardly a time when I visited Gabi, my close friend and neighbour, that he did not, in one way or another, make a reference to or narrate parts or the whole story of his father and the loss of their home in West Jerusalem. And there was hardly a time when Gabi's voice, and tears, did not fail him. This was hard, not only because Gabi, or Dr Baramki as most referred to him, was in a way my boss as the president of Briziet University where I taught, but also because it is often difficult to deal with someone's personal traumas, losses and pains when they happen to be yours as well.

Gabi was the eldest son of the renowned architect Andoni Baramki. Perhaps it was the fact that I was an architect myself that encouraged him to tell me the story again and again. Or was it I who kept probing Gabi for more, more and more?

My dear Gabi, now that you have departed from our martial world, all I can say is:

May you rest in peace, knowing that your story will be told and retold as many times as you wanted it to be.

2.

The Smile

Andoni Baramki (far right)
Also pictured, from left to right: Andoni's brother and sister-in-law
and their child; his mother, Khariklia; and his wife, Evelyn
Jerusalem, circa 1930
Courtesy of Haifa Baramki

T HERE SEEM TO HAVE been no disasters, natural or otherwise, the year Andoni was born.

It wasn't 1898, the year of the five harsh snowstorms.

Nor was it 1915, the year of the locusts.

Nor 1927, the year of the destructive earthquake.

Not even a war or an uprising.

The faded Arabic inscription on his gravestone in Ramallah's Christian Orthodox cemetery reads:

Andoni Jubra'il Ya'qub Baramki
Born in Jerusalem (January 1894)
Died in Ramallah (September 1972)
14 km away from his beloved

Next to Andoni's gravestone is his wife's:

Evelyn Khouri-Baramki
Born in Jaffa (April 1906)
Died in Ramallah (June 2004)
44 km away from her beloved hometown of Jaffa

Twelve years seemed to be the appropriate age difference between the well-established architect-groom and his bride.

His year of birth was calculated from her birth certificate.

This made sense to him. It made sense to her.

And to everyone around them.

Birth year established: 1894.

Name

Andoni's ageing half-Greek mother, Khariklia (not sounding too nice in Arabic, hence Farha), who lived with him and his family, or more accurately, they lived with her, called him Andoni with an accentuated 'd'. Evelyn, his good-natured and humorous wife, sometimes called him Toni, with a long 'iii' for intimacy (*dala*).

His Greek friends and classmates at the Academy of Fine Arts in Athens, including one who became the Benedictus (the Greek Orthodox Patriarch) of Jerusalem, called him Andonaiki.

Andoni, Toni or Andonaiki were all names for the same saint: Mar Anton, aka St Anthony, who is celebrated in January every year by all Jerusalem Christians, as well as Christians elsewhere in Palestine and Greater Syria. He, like all other Andonis, considered his saint's name-day as his own birthday. Hence the day on which our Andoni was biologically born remains unknown.

Birth month established: January 1894.

That smile

Andoni had a subtle smile: elusive, mysterious, restrained, abstract, ambiguous and indefinable. That smile was the most prominent feature of his well-defined face: a big round head, a big round nose, big protruding blue eyes and fleshy lips. It was difficult to figure out or explain what that enigmatic smile was about.

Khariklia, his mother, thought the innocent smile reflected a kind heart.

Evelyn, his wife, thought the adorable smile reflected a joyful husband.

His friends thought the peaceful smile reflected *saber* Ayyoub, the patience of Job, a tolerant and sincere friend.

But no one, not even his mother, could recall whether Andoni was born with that smile or whether he had slowly acquired it to reflect a life of varied experiences. Unlike the year and month in which he was born, the date that peculiar smile appeared was never established.

Work

It took the devastating earthquake of 1927 for people to real- ise the similarity between Andoni and his buildings: both were well-built and structurally sound. While numerous buildings in Jerusalem and other cities were badly damaged, all of Andoni's buildings stood proud.

So did he.

That catastrophic earthquake generated numerous archi- tectural projects for the master architect, his Jewish draftsman Abraham Cherniak and foreman Ginsburg, a German immi- grant who changed his name to Ben Hurin in 1949.

From the year of the earthquake onwards, Andoni's secular and religious projects spread all over Palestine, in cities and villages alike, until his death in 1972.

Though a well-known Christian Orthodox, Andoni's reputation convinced various churches, including the Latin Patriarchate in Jerusalem, to transcend sectarianism and seek his help and protection – in addition to that of the Virgin Mary, of course.

For the Latin Patriarchate in Jerusalem, Andoni built St

Joseph School in the Old City, the beautiful Romanian Church and convent near the Jewish neighbourhood of Mea She'arim, and little chapels at the Baptism Site on the banks of the Jordan River. He also designed buildings in Ramallah, the small and lovely summer resort where in 1927 he had met his beloved Evelyn. There he built the Sam'an Daoud House, the Kassis house, today's Hotel Casa Nova – its original design totally mutilated by 1980 additions – and the Aruri house, also known as the Mukhtar's house, in the village of Burham.

While the world was suffering from an economic depression in the late 1920s and 1930s, Jerusalem was witnessing a construction boom. Whole neighbourhoods, mansions, villas and apartment buildings were mushrooming on the hilly landscape around the Old City. Andoni's villas were the icing on the cake. His buildings sprang up in the new residential neighbourhoods: the Greek and German Colonies, Musrara, Sa'ed o Said, Katamon, Talbiyah and Upper and Lower Baq'a. A drive along the Jerusalem-Bethlehem road created the impression that Andoni was the only architect in town. 'Baramki style' became the term to describe buildings distinguished by the use of the Jerusalem pink stone, *slayyeb*, highlighted by the white stone he often used for the round and pointed arches.

The boom suggested that people built one villa to live in and another to rent out – or if economic means allowed, a complete apartment building. This was exactly what he did for himself and his family in 1929 and 1932: he built one splendid villa in the Sa'ed o Said area and another across the road in the posh neighbourhood of Musrara – a masterpiece that he always referred to as '*nour hayati*', the light of my life.

'You are the light of my life.'

But, as we all know, happiness and the good life never last long in the Holy Land, so as fighting between Arabs and Jews intensified in the spring of 1948, the Baramki family like thousands of other Palestinians, were forced to abandon their beautiful home and prosperous neighbourhood.

An orange cake and a knife to cut it with were all that Evelyn grabbed as the family frantically rushed out of the door. Everything happened in a panic following a bullet that grazed Evelyn's light brown hair. 'That's it!' shouted Andoni as he broke a promise that he had made to himself never to leave his home. But escape was their only choice as bullets rained through the shattering glass.

A hot orange cake in a hot baking tin.

A knife.

House keys.

These became mementoes of a distant past.

Andoni, Evelyn, Laura, sixteen, and George, thirteen, raced out of that house; the eldest son, Gabi, was away in Lebanon. The family would never be allowed into the house again.

To his misfortune, the light of his life ended up on the border of what had become Jewish West Jerusalem, less than a kilometre away from what became Arab East Jerusalem. The Israeli army on the western side, and the Jordanian army on the eastern side, like the two villas, faced one another.

The Baramki villas, Andoni's.

So close to his heart and eyes.

So unreachable.

Longing

Jerusalem 1948–1967

It was a crisp Saturday and the sun was setting
Like most other Saturdays, it was time for him to venture
  forth
He was apprehensive today, as he had been last Saturday
As he will be the following Saturday
From one war to another
He has been at it for nineteen years
From the 1948 war till the 1967 war
With a tiny difference:
With each new Saturday melancholy and grief intensified
Until death forced them apart
He looked left
He looked right
Then ducked his head
Bent his two-metre tall robust body
And swiftly sneaked into the stairway
None of his friends or the YMCA staff saw him vanish
Or so he thought
Or so they pretended
In spite of everything he still took the risk
To be the talk of the town
Or be caught or even shot at
And all that came with it:
The embarrassment of his three kids
The jealousy of his beautiful wife
And the reprimand of his mother
Love was stronger
A love that turned into a lifelong obsession

With the lightness of an Arab horse he elegantly trotted
  up the stairs
And in no time he was at the top of the four-storey
  stairway
And in no time he was face to face with the barrier he
  hated most:
The heavy and rusty iron gate that never failed to reveal
  to the enemy as well as the beloved the arrival of the
  crazed, the possessed.

He leaned his robust body against the cold surface of the
metal door, pushing at its rusty latch with his sturdy oversized
palms. He stood perfectly still until autumn clouds absorbed
the amplified clank of the latch and the deafening squeak of
the rusted hinges. Then and only then did he venture out
onto the open roof of the building.

Every Shabat, at sunset, the roof of the YMCA, like all
adjacent roofs, was completely deserted. This he knew from
past experience. But for extra caution, once in the open, he
ducked his head and, stooping, almost crawled towards the
western side of the roof.

Like a child he crouched behind the white stone parapet
and stiffly stretched his long legs on the dirty roof. He rested
his big head against the parapet and then, only then, took a
deep breath. Andoni did his breathing exercises three times a
week: once on the roof of this building and twice as the *basso
profundo* of the Jerusalem Orthodox Choir. As much as he
would have loved to sing for her on the occasion of their
Saturday encounters, he kept his desire under control.

Having regained his energy and steadied his heartbeat,
Andoni was ready for his weekly encounter.

He knelt down, straightened his shoulders, lifted his head above the parapet, and carefully looked over it. The second he saw her, tears formed and shone in his big blue eyes.

How much he missed her, how much he loved her
How much he treasured her white and pink complexion
The soft light reflecting on an even softer, undulating body
He admired everything about her
Her shape
Her form
Her movements
Her flawless proportions
The delightful floral ornaments
Everything about her was perfect
Every time he saw her or got close to her he surrendered his soul to the creator
Oh God, how beautiful she is
Tears ran down his cheek as he waved goodbye
She looked back at him, moaning softly
Then she smiled
He smiled back and walked away
Until next Saturday
Until the 1967 war
When he and his beloved were united once but not for all
Wars separate, others unite

Ramallah
Tuesday, 6 June
Second day of the 1967 war

The piercing shrieks of the fighter planes over the skies of
Ramallah made Andoni and Evelyn think the planes had
just rocketed through their bedroom. Their daughter,
Laura, son, Gabi, and his wife, Haifa, felt the same. They
all ran out of their respective bedrooms to the semi-
protected corridor.

Andoni's five grandchildren – Naila, Nadim, Hala, Hania
and Maha – expressed their fright by either wetting themselves or crying for hours on end. 'Baba . . . Baba . . . *biddi*
Babaaaa,' cried three-year-old Maha in search of her father,
Dr Abdallah, who had been stationed at a Bethlehem hospital
ever since the war erupted. That was why Laura and the four
children had taken refuge in her parents' house in Ramallah,
away from their home in Jerusalem. On the other hand, in
Haifa's womb, no one could tell how foetus Hani reacted to
the planes. Haifa could not distinguish between her fearful
heartbeats and her baby's fierce kicks.

The Baramkis, like everyone else, hoped that the hostili-
ties, which had begun early in the morning of the day before,
would move west in the direction of Israel. But the F16s left
them in no doubt that sleeping in their bedrooms on the
ground floor was not safe. Shortly after, mattresses were laid
on the cement floor of the unfinished basement of the house
Andoni had built five years earlier.

While everyone, including the smiling seventy-three-year-
old Andoni, was busy moving furniture, helping to modify
the living and sleeping arrangements for wartime, sweet and

unruffled Evelyn carried on with her stress-free daily routine. Business as usual.

Together with four of her grandchildren, she went for a short walk in the surrounding terraced olive groves, followed by a coffee break with one of the neighbours.

Had Ramallah not been under curfew, and had the bus passed by that morning, she would have taken her grandchildren to visit Aunt Linda, a sister of hers, who lived in the neighbouring town of Birzeit.

To divert the shell-shocked grandchildren and give Laura a break from her kids, Evelyn took them for a longer walk than usual. Once out of their mother's sphere of jurisdiction, Evelyn let go of the children's hands. She set them and herself free. While they frolicked in the empty streets of Ramallah, Grandma Evelyn sang at the top of her voice. Like everyone else in her family she had a beautiful and sensuous voice. It took the little children some time to realise that the high-pitched sounds that filled the skies above them did not originate from their grandmother's soprano but from the Israeli fighter planes.

Suddenly, the heavy-set grandmother and the little ones were running in terror as the F16 jets bombed targets close-by. They ran and ran; they ran and screamed; they screamed and tumbled to the ground, until the children were met by their hysterical mother.

Once Laura was wrapped protectively over her four kids, her reprimanding screams started and would not end, joining the cacophony of the Israeli fighter planes. When they rejoined the rest of the family in the congested basement, Evelyn became the bombing target in a family war that started then, but never ended.

Some screamed forever
Some cried forever
Some got depressed forever
Some, like Andoni, had a laughing fit
Which turned into an eternal cynical smile.

Even when Israeli soldiers came the next day, banging at his door and demanding the keys to Gabi's brand new Peugeot, Andoni continued to smile as he handed the keys over. Off the soldiers went on a sinister two-day mission. When they brought back the wreck of a car, Andoni walked around examining it. He took the keys and flashed his smile at them in return.

10 June 1967

Curfews were prolonged.

War nights were also prolonged.

Not only for the smiling old man, but also for the baby in Haifa's womb.

In spite of all the havoc around him, or perhaps because of it, little Hani was curious and hence determined to make it into the noisy world. He kicked and jerked until his mother, Haifa, and his father, Gabi, drove their bashed-up car under fire to the French Hospital in East Jerusalem. That same day, Friday, 10 June, little Hani was pulled out of his mother's womb and into a world of continuous action.

Andoni's striking smile grew more pronounced by the day, despite yet another defeat, which resulted in the occupation of the rest of Palestine: East Jerusalem, the West Bank and Gaza Strip, as well as Syria's Golan Heights and Egypt's Sinai desert, and led to the displacement of more Palestinians.

None of his family asked about his expression, nor did he explain.

'Come on kids, gather your things, we're going back home to Jerusalem!' Dr Abdallah assertively announced as he hugged his wife. Laura cried. No one could figure out why she cried; it may have been happiness or exhaustion, or perhaps both.

While the little children excitedly gathered their scattered toys and clothes, Grandpa Andoni rushed to his study.

Making sure to shut the door behind him, Andoni opened and closed all the drawers in his room as quickly as possible. He then went through the neatly organised folders, the many old photo albums, some documents, and finally unrolled and rolled back some architectural drawings.

In no time he was standing by the front door, neatly dressed and ready to go. The size of the red file he hugged close to his chest, as well as the luggage next to him, gave the impression that he was leaving and never coming back. And when his sweetheart Evelyn asked, 'Toniii, *habibi*, where are you going?'

He replied with an unwavering smile. 'I'm going to visit my beloved.'

'Your beloved?' she exclaimed, then added, 'Ah, you mean Hani, our new grandchild!'

Hesitantly he responded, 'Oh yes, Hani, our beloved new grandson.'

Relieved, she helped him out. He had forgotten about the family anxiety and that fearful and spooky drive Gabi and Haifa had taken in their battered car under curfew.

'But where, how will you see him?' It occurred to her to ask.

'I'm going to Jerusalem with Abdallah.'

'Toniii! You aren't serious, I hope! Abdallah came to take

Laura and the kids home, he didn't come to take you on a picnic. His car's full, but more importantly, I need you to be here with me and Hania.'

Toni only stood there, smiling.

'And why this big smile?' It was the first time anyone had commented on Andoni's enigmatic smile. Getting no response, Evelyn continued, 'And you know well enough that Gabi and Haifa will not be back with little Hani for another week or so.'

Her words fell on deaf ears.

Like a small child, Andoni ran to take the front seat, then stuck his head and part of his ample trunk out of the window. 'I need to see everything,' he announced.

'See what? All the destruction in Jerusalem?' Dr Abdallah asked as he loaded the trunk with all the family luggage.

'Was there much destruction around the YMCA building?' Andoni asked, holding the red file tightly against his chest.

Laura smiled while her husband replied, 'Andoni, I'm not sure. I, like you, have been stuck under curfew, but from the news I gathered that the fighting was mostly concentrated around the seam-line: Jabal al-Mukabber and the Mandelbaum Gate next to the YMCA area.'

'Around the YMCA!' Andoni repeated, then pressed his big palm to his forehead.

The destruction around the YMCA area caused the adults to fall into a long silence which lasted the whole trip from Ramallah to Jerusalem.

'Off I go,' declared Andoni as soon as they reached his daughter's house, slamming the car door behind him. He hugged his four grandchildren first, then his daughter, and then Abdallah.

'Good bye, Jiddo,' Nadim and his sisters called out.

'Take care, Baba, please don't do anything silly like Mama!' Laura said, referring to Evelyn's hazardous walk with the kids. Then Laura and Abdallah dashed into their deserted house with the kids in tow.

'Forgot your suitcase!' Abdallah yelled after Andoni.

'I'll come back for it,' he replied, looking back and waving his hand as his legs picked up speed.

Laura had already figured out that once that smile appeared on her Baba's face it meant that he was lost in his own world. In a trance he walked into the city and, in the same state, talked his way past civilians and soldiers alike to the western side of the seam-line.

He was so determined that no one dared to challenge his urgent need to get some place and meet someone he had neither seen nor touched in almost two decades. Separation made it feel more like two centuries.

Love, war and trauma create a peculiar sense of time.

Andoni's pounding eager steps, the pumping of his accelerated heartbeat, the jingling of his keys as well as the sporadic shooting around him composed the background music, a symphony, to the lovers' encounter. The closer he got to her, the more dramatically the symphony echoed in his ears until there was a sudden silence.

Everything froze once he was face to face with his beloved. He smiled, she smiled back at him.

He stretched out his arms towards her.

And then a man with a gun appeared from behind, and in a not-so-friendly fashion challenged, yelled and threatened, cursed and turned violent, finally brandishing his rifle and threatening to kill Andoni.

43

And that pulled the lovers apart once again.

In the years that followed, a solitary Andoni stood at a safe distance and stared at his beloved: the light of his life.

One small detail
Courtroom
October 1968

That morning Andoni had woken up early, even though he hadn't slept much. He was clean-shaven and elegantly dressed. The dark navy-blue suit he had carefully picked for the occasion made him look like a shrewd businessman rather than the casual yet tasteful architect that he was. The fat red file held close to his heart reflected the same degree of attention to detail.

Being positive and optimistic were two of Andoni's virtues, in addition to being patient – very patient, extremely patient. Patience was a distinctive quality of this branch of the Baramki family.

Many had been sceptical, some decidedly so, about Andoni's appeal to the enemy's courts in West Jerusalem. But love knows no boundaries, nor do Israeli courts. There was Andoni's two-metre-tall body jumping up and down with joy, now that the Israeli court had indeed issued an eviction order against the Jewish squatter who had occupied his house: his rival with the gun.

Everything now seemed possible, so Andoni spent most of the family savings to hire the renowned Israeli lawyer Avraham Ronen.

Not only had Ronen previously won an eviction case, he had recently also won a case in which a Palestinian family, the Tazzeez, were allowed back to live in their house on the eastern side of the seam-line, the 1949 Armistice Line. The Tazzeez house in Sa'ed o Said neighbourhood was once Andoni's own house; he had been forced to sell it when in 1945 his business went bankrupt. Despite this reminder of a sad chapter in his life, he was in seventh heaven about a rare case in which an Arab family had won the right to move back to their own house.

Andoni stood tall next to his assertive lawyer in the Israeli courtroom. As agreed, Ronen read a few introductory notes to remind the judge that this was only 'a follow-up' on an already won case.

'Your Honour, thanks to the judgement of this court, now that the occupier of Architect Andoni's house has been evicted, my client is seeking a court ruling that would allow him to go home.' Ronen smiled at Andoni and added, 'Mr Baramki, I hope you do not mind me calling you by your first name?'

Surprised by this unnecessary interruption, Andoni smiled back nervously at his lawyer, who then carried on. 'Well, Your Honour, we are seeking your respected court's permission to allow Mr Baramki and his family to go back and live in their home in the Musrara neighbourhood.'

Andoni was thrilled to hear the words 'Mr Baramki and his family to go back and live in their home'. His eyes sparkled. He also liked the use of the word 'occupier' with reference to the Israeli squatter. If he succeeded in getting this small occupier out of his house perhaps he could eventually get the big Occupier out of his country. One thing at a time, he thought to himself.

'Well, Your Honour, in the fifty years of my long professional life, and of all that I have designed and built – houses, villas, apartment buildings, churches, hotels, office buildings

– this happens to be my favourite. In all modesty, it is a masterpiece. I love it as much as I love my children and grand-children, perhaps even more. You know what I call it? *Nour hayati*, and you know, Your Honour, what *nour hayati* means in Arabic? This villa in particular was . . .'

The judge interrupted. 'Of course I understand Aghabic and what *nour hayati* means, but Architect Baramki you can't possibly love a house or a villa more than you love your children. No, *Bash Muhandis* (honourable architect), that is neither possible nor appropriate.' The judge affirmed his moral position on the issue.

To gain the judge's sympathy Andoni opted to justify his love, his obsession, by stepping forward and handing the judge a huge photo album of his splendid villa. The dated photos covering the years from 1948 to 1967 were all taken from a bird's eye view.

'Indeed, it is a gorgeous villa. You Arabs know how to build beautiful houses. I myself live in an Arab house,' said the judge, smiling approvingly.

Andoni smiled back, while thinking to himself: Not only did you take the whole of Palestine and all Palestinian prop-erty – our towns, villages, farms, orange groves, children's schools and playgrounds, hospitals, offices and banks; our markets, shops, big and small, buses, cars, seashores and boats; our cattle, sheep, camels, dogs, cats, chickens, donkeys, and our beautiful Arab horses; my architectural practice, my beau-tiful villa, my lush green gardens, my furniture, my piano, my Persian carpets, my books, my children's beds and toys, my mother's crochet box and novels and my wife's paintings and music books; our kitchen appliances and utensils: fridge, oven, water kettle, cutlery, cups, plates; and all my family photo albums – and yet you still have the effrontery to brag about it. 'I myself live in an Arab house!' Shameless!

Of course, a respected judge like yourself, like many other high-ranking government officials, army generals and senior officers, in return for kicking us out, were all offered Arab houses in Arab neighbourhoods. Even your Golda Meir lived in an Arab house. Ask me, Judge, and I will tell you in whose house your respected Prime Minister lived. She also bragged about living in Harun al-Rashid's villa in the German Colony. Ask me and I will tell you that her villa belonged to our friends, the Bisharat family. Ask me, Judge, I know them, each and every one. Would Your Honour like a list of those of you who live in Arab houses that I built? And whose house is it that you live in and brag about, Your Honour? And you have the guts to tell us, 'Ah, you must be Mr Dajani! Ah, you must be Mr Sakakini! Ah, you must be Mr Nammari! Ah, you must be Mr Baramki – because the water and electricity bills are still in your name.' Why don't you send us the phone bills, too, so that we pay them for you, Your Honour?

Andoni contained the anger mounting inside him. He was more concerned with his personal gains: he was simply seeking a court ruling that allowed him to live in his house.

'Is there anything else you want to say or present, Architect Baramki?' inquired the judge as he continued flipping through the photos of the beautiful Arab villa.

'Yes, Your Honour. Here is the land deed and here is the house title issued in 1932 when I completed work on the villa.' Andoni carefully handed the judge the well-preserved legal documentation certifying his ownership of the land and the villa built on it. To Andoni's utter surprise the judge showed extreme interest in the title. This made Andoni feel that substantiating his ownership had finally paid off.

'And where did you obtain this deed, Mr Baramki?' asked the judge.

'From the Jordanian Land Registry Office in Jerusalem.' Andoni was growing truly hopeful that he might be able to set the record straight, both for his own house and for Palestine as a whole. The more the judge examined the land deed, as he had done with the photo album, the louder Andoni's heart beat.

'Architect Baramki, you seem to be a rich man, but of course most architects are, they make a draft of your house and then a draft on your bank account!' The judge laughed so much it seemed it was the first time he had heard his own joke.

'Isn't that better than drafting your children into so many wars, Your Honour? How many of them so far?' It was not clear whether 'how many' referred to the number of wars or the number of children drafted. Now it was Andoni's turn to laugh at his own joke. Since Arabs and Israelis do not laugh at each other's jokes, each had to tell and laugh at his own.

'Mr Baramki, we are not here to talk politics. Let us stick to your case.'

'Then here are the blueprints for my house.' Andoni presented a large set of drawings that covered the judge's high podium.

A long pause followed, with neither one seeming to know where to go next. Then the judge spoke, looking Andoni straight in the eye. 'Well, Mr Baramki, the matter is obviously not that simple.'

'Not that simple! What is not that simple?' asked Andoni, taken aback.

'I mean to say,' the judge now addressed the lawyer, 'that I am sure both you and your client, Architect Baramki, realise that it is not a simple matter, Mr Baramki moving back into his house in Musrara.'

'Here are the house keys,' said Andoni, pulling out the bunch of keys he had carried in his pocket for the last twenty years. This brought a glimmer to his eyes, but he quickly reined in his emotions and continued. 'One week to white-wash and paint the house, another few days to clean it up, then a few truck-loads of furniture and my family and I would be settled back in our home. How much simpler could it be? It only needs your consent, sir.'

'Well, Mr Baramki, I wish it were that simple, but unfortunately it is not. It is not that simple,' he repeated, trying to placate Andoni. 'It is true that you have won the case for evicting the Jewish squatter from your house, but that does not automatically mean you can move there to live in it, just like that.'

Andoni only found hope in the judge saying 'your house', which was in itself an acknowledgement, and in his use of the word 'automatically', which could imply that while it was not automatic, it could still happen.

'Mr Baramki, I must compliment you on all the interesting documents, photos and drawings that you have kept of your house for all these years, and now the house keys, but I am afraid there is an important small detail that you seem to have missed . . . You are an absentee,' the judge declared after a pause.

'Absentee?' Andoni looked questioningly at his lawyer, who remained silent.

'Yes, as far as the law is concerned, you are an absentee.

49

You are an absentee landlord and consequently your house is absentee property.' Realising the absurdity of what he had just said the judge avoided looking at Andoni.

'Absent? Absent? How can I be absent?' Andoni kept repeating until he was interrupted.

'An absentee,' the judge corrected him.

'An absentee, how can I be an absentee when I am standing right in front of Your Honour?'

'Well, as I am sure Mr Ronen knows very well, as far as Israeli law is concerned you are an absentee landlord,' the judge coldly reiterated, addressing the Israeli lawyer over Andoni's protestations.

'But, sir, in this case, in my case, as you can very well see, neither I nor the house from which you evicted the squatter are absent.'

'Mr Baramki, I understand your frustration, but as I explained to you and to your lawyer, as far as Israeli law is concerned you are an absentee landlord, and hence your house is absentee property. There is nothing I can do about this fact.'

'Fact! I am an absentee landlord and my property is also absentee?' Andoni repeated in disbelief.

Sensing Andoni's anger the judge added, 'It's nothing personal, Mr Baramki; there are hundreds of thousands of Arabs who are considered absentees, just like you. All Palestinian refugees, whether present or absent, are considered absentees,' explained the judge.

'Sir, the Palestinians are "absentees" only because you do not allow them to be present. And those of us who are present are considered absent. We can never win.'

'True, some of you are physically here.'

'That "some of you" numbers hundreds of thousands, sir.'

'Yes, I know. With all due respect, it's nothing personal, Bash Muhandis.'

Andoni opened and closed his two large fists, stretched ten long fingers, and then started beating them against his body, as if reassuring himself that it was present and accounted for. He began pounding his chest, picking up speed and force, then moved downwards to his stomach, abdomen, and upper thighs, all the while chanting, to the triple beat of his drumming fingers: 'Ab-sen-tee, ab-sen-tee, ab-sen-tee!'

'Well, in this case you are both present and absent at the same time. You belong to the "present absentee" category,' said the judge.

'Is this a philosophical, existential matter, sir?' Andoni asked incredulously, glancing at his lawyer. Though Andoni knew perfectly well that 'present absentee' was the Israeli legal status assigned to all Palestinians who stayed on their lands after the 1948 war, he could not grasp the fact that he remained 'an absentee' despite his presence in front of the judge.

The judge was clearly losing interest in the existential crisis he had provoked in Andoni, or for that matter in his essential existence altogether. Meanwhile, Andoni's smile was widening. It seemed to pull the judge back in so he said, 'No, Mr Baramki, this is not philosophical, it is the law, Israeli law.'

Andoni thought it best to let go of all existentialist arguments at least for the time being – opting instead for a commonly used line of argument that all Palestinians, and Israelis for that matter, use to win any debate. 'Sir, I am from Jerusalem. I was born in Jerusalem, as were my father and my grandfather and my great-great-grandfather. I was raised in Jerusalem; I live in Jerusalem; I worked in Jerusalem; I got married in Jerusalem; I raised my family in Jerusalem and built many buildings and houses in Jerusalem, in Jerusalem . . . in Jerusalem . . .'

Having heard this argument so many times the judge began to yawn.

Realising that historical facts did not resonate with Israeli judges, Andoni shifted to logic and common sense. 'Your Honour, why is it that when it comes to paying taxes to the Israeli government you do not consider us absentees, but when it comes to getting our property back then we are considered absentees? No one ever told me you are an absentee hence you should not pay the *arnona*.' (*Arnona* is a Hebrew word for taxes that has almost become an Arabic word as a result of the incredible amount of taxes East Jerusalem Arabs pay.)

The judge had almost dozed off. Catching himself about to snore, he shook his head, straightened his posture and addressed Baramki in a tone that indicated he wished to conclude the matter. 'Well, Mr Baramki, I am afraid that is the law.'

'Which law? What law, sir?' Andoni was growing desperate.

'What law? Israeli law, of course.'

'If Israeli law rules that I am an absentee when I am standing right in front of Your Honour, then what does Your Honour say about that?'

'I, of course, follow the law,' replied the judge.

'And who made this law, sir?' asked Andoni. 'The government.'

'Sir, do you see a human being in front of you? Or do you only hear the voice of a ghost?'

'Do you think I am blind?' the judge fired back. 'Case dismissed.' He rose abruptly, walked out of the room and shut the door behind him.

The Israeli lawyer escorted absentee Andoni out of the courtroom.

Andoni stood in the court lobby staring at all those around him gathered there to seek Israeli justice.

Soon his smile turned into giggles
His giggles into chuckles
He could no longer hold back his laughter
He first rolled with laughter
Then bent over
Holding his stomach, then his abdomen
Soon he rolled on the floor, on his back, feet up and
    kicking in the air
Laughter filled the air
There was laughter, more laughter, and still more
    laughter
Until the laughter subsided
Then there was silence
More silence until
Silence prevailed
Stillness prevailed
Dead silence prevailed.

3.

Museum of Tolerance and Co-existence

The Baramki House
Musrara, West Jerusalem, 1972
Courtesy of the late Dr Gabi Baramki

Those who have children never die. (*Illi khallaf ma mat*)

Arabic proverb

Gabi: Andoni's eldest son

12 June 1983 was a Sunday
He, like everyone else, stood in line
The queue was long
Like his father, he was patient
So he waited
Soon he found himself in the midst of a turbulent ocean:
An animated, loud crowd of young men and women
A bit irritated
Still he waited
What was I like at their age? he asked himself
A moment for contemplation

At their age, at eighteen

In October 1946, almost eighteen, Gabi, like them, was very keen to learn about the world. He wanted to go beyond the boundaries of a protective family and a wounded country. Beirut, the jewel of the Arab world with its American University, was his goal.

In April 1948, during Gabi's second year at the University, he found himself cut off from both family and homeland. He waited many restless days, long sad months and an endless year to re-unite with his family. It was summer 1949 in the city of Gaza.

'An orange cake, but no family albums!' protested Gabi, tears filling his big brown eyes as he suddenly realised that he

56

had lost his past, his childhood and his teenage memories. There was no proof that he had ever had a life in Jerusalem; there was no way home.

A photo album meant existence.

But all he could do at that moment was to vow not to eat orange cake ever again.

At their age, almost eighteen

At their age I was on the shores of Lebanon, Gabi thought to himself again. No, he was not swimming or sunbathing, as first fantasised. Together with his teenage friends, he was lending a hand in pitching tents and setting up refugee camps.

The exodus from Palestine to Lebanon had brought thousands of refugees. Like waves they had arrived, and like waves their spirits and aspirations had crashed against the reality of their new lives as their crowded boats ground ashore.

Gabi had found himself face to face with his uncle, Wadi Khouri. With him – Gabi could hardly believe his eyes – were Aunt Salma and their children, Toni, Eliana and Zahi. Their other daughter, Fifi, with her husband and two-year-old daughter were also there. They had fled the heavily bombarded city of Jaffa.

As more and more refugees stepped off the boats on the shores of the Mediterranean, more were arriving on foot. Yes, on foot. But whichever way they arrived, none had an inkling of what to do next, or where to go.

At their age, at eighteen, Gabi, like the rowdy young people around him, must have been strong: thirty-five years later the temporary wooden posts that he and his sturdy friends had planted deep in Lebanese soil had turned into permanent concrete poles.

As permanent as the refugees' sense of estrangement, and as deep as their sense of loss, which remained with them wherever they spread:

To the shores of Lebanon

To Syria's many oases

To the flooded river banks of Cairo and Baghdad

To Jordan's plains and deserts

To the hot sand dunes of Kuwait, Saudi Arabia and the Arab Gulf

To Tunis and Libya

To this Arab capital or that

To sub-Saharan Africa

To Paris, to New York

To Havana, Rio de Janeiro, Santiago

They dispersed

In exile.

And now Gabi, at fifty-three, was patiently waiting in line for the grand opening of a new museum in Jerusalem. No more reflections on an unfortunate and sad past.

Live the moment, he instructed himself.

While everyone around him, young and old, locals and tourists, chatted and giggled, his silence deepened; a knot formed in his chest. With every slow step closer to the museum, Gabi's anxiety increased. *What is it?* he asked himself.

Everything about the crowd around him made him sad, very sad:

Their laid-back attitude

Their joyfulness

The little anecdotes and quips
The mundane topics of their chatter
Their indifference to it all
Especially to his pain
The simple things in life that they took for granted
The normality of their lives.

That's what got to him most: they were acting like normal people in a normal country. And this reminded him of his and his people's great losses.

Only then did he realise what he missed the most: a mundane life. He missed having a normal life.

Yes, it was normality that he missed most.

'For God's sake, stop it!' Gabi yelled at two teenage boys who interrupted his daydream, or rather nightmare. They were shoving one another. He turned back and stared at them. He then checked the queue.

It was still long. So he waited.

Realising that neither justice nor normality were around the corner, Gabi decided to unwind. He pulled the new museum's brochure out of a file. The design was rather weak and unattractive, he thought. Not to mention its content:

THE TOURJEMAN POST
For a better understanding of Jerusalem's recent history
Overlooking the former mandelbaum gate area, the Tourjeman post was a frontier position during the period when Jerusalem was divided (1948–1967) it has now been restored and is dedicated to the theme: Jerusalem – a divided city reunited

permanent exhibition
observation terrace
audio-visual programme
video films
reference library
open: Sunday–Thursday, 9 am–4 pm Friday 9 am–1 pm
Chail Handassa st. 4 tel. 281278
buses 1, 11, 27, 99

To him it was obvious that the light blue colour of the brochure recalled the Israeli flag, but they could have chosen a more interesting shade of blue. He wasn't impressed by the quality of paper either. But worst of all were the layout and the many typos. The latter truly got to him. As president of Birzeit University, Dr Gabi Baramki always read and re-read every single university publication. He made sure not to allow any typo to escape his scrutiny.

Gabi carried on with his impossible editorial mission: Mandelbaum and Gate should start with capital letters: *Overlooking the former mandelbaum gate*, it read. He gazed at the word 'former' and wondered how many of the Israeli young-sters realised that the queue in which they were standing right now delineated the divide between East and West Jerusalem. *The Green Line, which far from being green, is rather dusty*, he mused. This 'No Man's Land' which actually belonged to many Palestinian families, all of whom Gabi knew and could name. Even the choice of name for the first Israeli checkpoint, the Mandelbaum Gate, was partial. But he decided not to dwell on the fact that the name came from the only Jewish house in the midst of an Arab neighbourhood. *Perhaps the only neutral term to use is 'The 1949 Armistice Line'*, Gabi thought to himself.

For nineteen years the Mandelbaum Gate provided the only access between the two parts of the divided city. This was where divided Palestinian families – those who remained in what became Israel and those who were forced to flee – had their annual family reunions. Yes, while families around the world had their family reunions in exciting places such as Paris, Rome, or on the lovely shores of Greece or the Caribbean islands, Palestinian family reunions took place on an Armistice Line crossing, at a checkpoint called the Mandelbaum Gate.

Gabi recalled the exchange of presents between his relatives. While Uncle Hanna and Aunt Victoria brought fresh fish from the seaport of Jaffa, Gabi's parents carried small coffee cups. As Israeli fast mud coffee slowly replaced the leisurely boiled Arabic coffee spiced with cardamom, it was becoming increasingly difficult to find the small Arabic coffee cups in the market.

Gabi realised at this point that these rowdy teenagers in the queue had been mere toddlers during the 1967 war, not to mention the 1948 one. These kids were the same age as his daughter, Hania, and his son, Hani. Of course! It was only two days ago, 10 June, that Hani had celebrated his sixteenth birthday. Gabi vividly recalled how, during the 1967 war, he had had to rush his wife, Haifa, to a Jerusalem hospital in a bashed-up car, violating curfew in order to deliver Hani in Jerusalem so he could have a Jerusalem birth certificate.

This realisation made him see these kids in a new light; he should at least give them credit for waiting that long in line to see the new museum. Especially as none of his children had agreed to accompany him, not even his youngest, Sami. These kids had a long wait ahead of them to learn about tolerance and co-existence.

From the fat red file he inherited from his father, Gabi pulled out a few more clippings. Ever since he had first heard of the museum and its grand opening he had started collecting all the published material he could find on the subject. He had clippings from different magazines and newspapers in Hebrew, Arabic, English, French and German, the language of Georg von Holtzbrinck, the publisher whose generous gift made this museum a reality.

As the queue started moving, Gabi's skimming through the clippings got faster, his eyes jumping from one line under-lined in red to another:

THE TOURJEMAN POST
The story of the period, and the history of Jerusalem as a divided city are well preserved in the Tourjeman Post . . . This house, now a museum, was once the last Israeli outpost overlooking the convoys on their way to Mt Scopus. Some of the bullet holes in the walls still remain. The narrow, armour-plated windows are witness to nineteen years of Jordanian snipers firing at Israeli houses across the border fence.

A photo of the museum building accompanied the last review. Gabi stared at the photo and looked up. From where he was standing it was difficult to see the bullet holes; however, he clearly saw the bombarded front façade and the blown-up arches of the two balconies, as well as the cement-blocked windows.

The damage was not repaired: it was preserved by an Israeli deci-sion as a witness . . . A witness to what? Gabi wondered.

In 1948 the Hagana seized the building to use it as a forward military position.

It was used by the IDF as an observation post . . . Could this war-scarred building become a symbol of understanding?

Gabi pondered the same question.

As the queue finally started moving quickly, Gabi flipped through a few more pages:

The Museum, the first of its kind in Israel. Dedicated to dialogue, understanding and coexistence. A meeting point, a place to clarify and discuss questions concerning war, peace, conflict and reconciliation.

Gabi was getting a bit confused about the museum's name, spelled variously in different articles, and given altogether different names in others: The Tourjeman Post, The Tourjeman House, The Turjeman Position, The Tourjeman Museum, The Unification of Jerusalem Museum, The Peace Museum, Museum of Co-existence, Reconciliation Museum, and Museum on the Seam.

He knew how to spell his friend's name: Hassan BekTurjman. Even though the 'man' ending of the name made it sound Jewish, the Turjmans were an Arab family. Perhaps that was why the Israelis opted for this name. *Turjman* in Arabic meant 'translator'. But most importantly, Gabi knew well that this was certainly not a Turjman Post. And he also knew that historical accuracy was never Israel's forte.

Just before Gabi put everything back into the file to move along with the queue, he read parts of an article written by one of the museum's former curators, Efrat Ben-Zeef:

Although it was rather obvious, it took me a while to realise that the whole idea of turning it into a museum of co-existence is naïve and impossible under the current circumstances.

Inside the new museum

Gabi could hear every step he took towards the new museum, a rhythm: *boom . . . boom . . . boom . . . boom . . .* Gabi, like his father Andoni, sang bass in the Jerusalem Choir.

A numbness was stealing over his entire body as he ascended the steps of the three-arched balcony; excessive sweating spotted his elegant white shirt. He contemplated leaving the building at once. Not after this painfully long wait, he convinced himself.

A few more steps and Gabi found himself inside the entrance lobby. He felt he was drowning in the crowd of bodies, loud speeches in Hebrew emanating from speakers seeming to wash over him.

He shuddered, then froze. He felt dizzy, his eyes moving faster than his brain. His head was pounding. Not only because of the animated youngsters who were still pushing against him from behind, but also because of the loud and poor quality of the amplified Hebrew speeches and the deafening applause that followed and filled the hall. Even though he understood some Hebrew, he could hardly make out the words that were hissing from the four loudspeakers stuck high up in the lobby's four corners.

A moment of despair

Gabi's eyes rested on the balustrade of the internal staircase. He took a deep breath and allowed his eyes to travel along the railing. The two gilded letters 'E' and 'A' were nicely incorporated within the beautiful wrought-iron design. Although Gabi was a chemist, he, like his late father, had an eye for architectural detail. He missed his father.

Gabi gazed at the ceiling of the lobby. He replaced the modern spotlights with a spring green and light rose Murano chandelier. He then looked to his left and changed the high-tech aluminium counter for a red mahogany desk and bookcase. He took two steps to one side of the long queue and stole a quick glance at the huge hall to the right. A glass screen separated the three bay windows from the great hall. What a pity, it would have been much better if the bay windows had remained part of the great hall, flooding it with light.

He removed the round glass table inside the bay window area in favour of a set of Chippendale white and beige sofas, two red leather Art Deco chairs and a mahogany coffee table. On the coffee table were two half-filled coffee cups and a stack of *National Geographic* and *Life* magazines. One was open to a photo of a beautiful black horse, probably an Arabian.

Gabi leaned forward, catching a glimpse of the three blown-up posters hanging on the opposite wall of the same hall. He read the bold lettering on each:

Photographs of the Divided and Reunited City (1948–67)

Paintings of Jerusalem

Poems about Jerusalem

Just before he finished replacing the three posters with portraits of family members and original still-life paintings, someone tapped him on the right shoulder.

'Could you get back in line?' Israelis do not have much use for the word 'please'. He mechanically complied. From his new position Gabi could now see another clearly legible sign:

The Room of Vision: Hertzel and Ben-Gurion

Why the additional 't' and 'e' in Hertzel? His name was Herzl, Gabi edited mentally. It was only at this point that he realised that the loud noise filling the entrance hall had come from The Room of Vision. The voice of Herzl, the father of Zionism, and the voice of Andoni, the father of both Gabi and modern architecture in Palestine, were echoing like a mixed track in his head. The Independence of Israel Speech by its first prime minister, David Ben-Gurion, and the echoing of the passionate words of Palestine's first architect drowned everything else.

Wedding of Gabi and Haifa Baramki by Greek Orthodox
Patriarch Benedictus
Mount of Olives, Jerusalem, 1963
Courtesy of Haifa Baramki

Behind the high-tech aluminium ticket counter hung a huge photo of a family that could almost have been Gabi's own. To the left of a round wooden table sat a bearded man and a woman, probably his wife, in a stylish white dress. Their two children, dressed elegantly, stood behind, the boy leaning against the table, the girl standing behind her dad.

Herzl and his family, c. 1866–1873

Gabi gazed at the Herzl family photo. No wonder they won the world's sympathy, they reflect so many human faces from countless family photo albums.

Gabi remembered the family albums left behind. He looked around frantically.

A moment of cold terror.

At the ticket counter

'How many tickets? One?' inquired the young woman sitting behind the high-tech aluminium counter.

'Tickets?' Gabi exclaimed, absentmindedly.

'Yes, tickets!' smiled back the ticket vendor.

'Tickets?' Gabi repeated.

'Yes, sir, tickets.' She smiled again, then cautiously asked, 'Senior?'

'Senior?' Gabi's face broke into a broad smile as he added, 'Perhaps too senior, exceedingly senior!'

'Come on . . . For God's sake, hurry up, buy the bloody ticket and move on!' complained a young voice behind him.

For a fraction of a second Gabi looked back, then turned and gazed at the ticket woman for long moments.

'Did you say I should buy a ticket?' Gabi came back to his theme.

'Yes, sir. This is not a free museum, you must buy a ticket, I don't understand the problem.' She was perplexed, a little annoyed.

'Must! Indeed. And how much is the ticket?' Gabi seemed

to ponder this deeply, the smile continuing to spread across his face.

'Thirty shekels regular, twenty-five for seniors.'

'Thirty shekels regular, twenty-five for seniors,' Gabi repeated.

The ticket woman lost her temper. 'What's the matter with you, sir? Today is the museum's opening, and as you can see we have tons of visitors waiting in line.' She rolled her eyes and sighed.

'Yes, yes, of course, what is the matter with me?' Gabi responded, his smile slowly turning into hysterical laughter.

'For fuck's sake, something is seriously wrong with this man, would someone get him out of the queue? How much longer are we expected to wait?' The complaints from the line behind him were getting louder and angrier.

'You want me to pay thirty shekels to enter . . . this is . . . my . . .' Gabi's attempts at speech were foiled by his hysterical laughter.

People stood there, watching nervously.

Gabi gave it another try. 'Do you really want me to pay thirty Israeli shekels to enter my hou . . . my family hou . . . The Baramki hou . . . my father, Andoni . . . Baramki . . .'

No one around him could figure out what he was trying to say.

'*Mazeh?* I don't understand what is going on here, sir.' The ticket clerk made one last attempt.

Gabi's obscure words were transformed into nervous howls: as loud and as deafening as those of Herzl and Ben-Gurion's Independence Day speeches.

He chuckled and laughed, then bent over clutching his stomach.

'I think he is saying this is his family's house!'

A moment of silence.

The ticket girl ducked down.

Some froze.

Some cautiously moved away.

Some ran out.

Some opted to shut their eyes.

But the vast majority closed their ears and carried on with their lives.

Business as usual.

Life as normal.

They acted like they were normal people in a normal country.

Gabi's laughter first filled the entrance hall, soon after travelled to the guest quarters, to the dining room, then to the huge kitchen. It made its way to the family room upstairs, into his parents' bedroom, his sister's pink bedroom, his brother's blue room and finally into his own. The laughter went into every drawer and into the corners of the closets in his room, but the photo albums were nowhere in sight.

To this day, museum visitors feel the reverberation of joyless laughter in the air.

A true account of the museum

From 28 April 1948, when the Baramkis left their home, until the grand opening of the Tourjeman Post Museum on 12 June 1983 – for thirty-five years, that is – none of the Baramkis had been able to set foot in their own house.

George Baramki, Gabi's younger brother, went to visit the 'museum' once. However their father, Andoni, the architect, had passed away eleven years earlier, in September 1972, and was never allowed in, never again saw 'the light of his life' from the inside. Evelyn, his wife and Gabi and George's mother, in whose name the house was registered, and their sister, Laura, could never bring themselves to stand in that 'museum' queue. Their tears would have flooded the whole of the Holy Land.

It was reported that the sponsor of the museum, Georg von Holtzbrinck, died in Germany on the night of the grand opening of the Tourjeman Post Museum.

Part Three
Huda

Peace – that was another name for home.

Kathleen Norris

Villa Bisharat, also known as Villa Harun al-Rashid,
where Israeli Prime Minister Golda Meir lived
Talbiyah, West Jerusalem, circa January 1928
Courtesy of Dr George Bisharat

4.

Golda Slept Here

November 2011

I T IS A BEAUTIFUL autumn day in Jerusalem. The very last thing that the two elegantly dressed ladies and I expect, on an outing on a spring-like day, is that one of us will be arrested, handcuffed and thrown into prison.

Nahil, seventy-eight, is Huda's older cousin. She has just arrived in Jerusalem from Damascus, via Amman and across the Allenby Bridge.

Hurriedly, Nahil checks into the American Colony Hotel, by far the most charming and expensive hotel in East Jerusalem. She could have taken time to freshen up, relax, have a nice cup of Turkish coffee, or even a drink in the hotel's splendid courtyard, but instead she opts to rush to her cousin's office in the Old City of Jerusalem. Attractive and wild-looking Huda is surprised and delighted to see her older cousin. The two exchange many warm kisses.

'Sorry, *habibti* Huda, I didn't mean to descend on you like *qadar*, fate, without warning, but the second Samir told me that our German Colony house was no longer occupied by the Jewish school, I came running.'

There is a nervy silence before Nahil adds, 'Imagine, today could be the day when I'll set foot inside our house again. I haven't been in it since I left in 1947. I recall that day as if it were yesterday: it was 13 September, a brisk and sunny day. I was so excited to get to my university in Damascus, I hadn't the slightest inkling that I'd never be able to come back home again.'

Nahil's eyes have a far-away look in them, as if she were already home.

Attempting to calm down her highly anxious and emotional cousin, Huda smiles and speaks in a very comforting tone. 'Relax, *habibti*, we'll go and see it right away. Your brother is right; it's no longer a school so there's no guard to prevent you from going in. It's now a construction site and will remain so for a while. I've already been there a number of times. I don't know if Samir told you, but Amidar has put the whole compound up for sale: yours, Uncle Subhi's and Teta Aysheh's.'

What a strange way to lower Nahil's high anxiety, I think, telling her that Amidar, the Israeli government agency entrusted with Arab 'absentee' properties, has decided to sell her family property.

'Up for sale?' Nahil is in total shock. She slaps the sides of her head with both hands while her jaw drops. She collapses into a chair and stares blankly for a long time. When she recovers she asks in a broken, shaky voice, 'And has Amidar already sold our houses?'

'I don't think so, *habibti*. I was there two weeks ago. Though the important thing for now is for you to get inside the house.' Huda seems to regret having given Nahil such bad news.

Nahil decides to focus on the good news for now. 'OK, let's go.' They both rise from their chairs.

Since Huda is leaving work earlier than usual, she stacks her

74

papers and then forces them into her soft leather black handbag.

Clickety-click, clickety-click . . .

Huda strides energetically down the corridor, swaying left and right, her high heels announcing the departure of the Director of the Centre for Jerusalem Studies at Al-Quds University. The domes of the renovated Turkish hammam seem to amplify, rather than absorb, the sound of Huda's footsteps.

Huda is as elegant as usual in her short grey skirt, black tights planted into high-heel boots, and a skin-tight grey blouse over which hangs a burgundy shawl. She always looks like she is on her way to one of the many receptions held by one or the other of the diplomatic missions in Jerusalem. In fact, she often goes to the French Consulate where her son, Hani, works. Both Huda and her son carry French passports acquired through Huda's previous marriage to a man from Martinique. Perhaps that is one source of Huda's incredible courage, verging on recklessness, in facing life in general and Israeli soldiers and authorities in particular.

Huda's fluffy, light-brown curls frame an ever-smiling face sitting atop an animated physique that radiates a confident personality and an attitude of entitlement. This makes her pass for a coquettish French woman, which no doubt helps her deceive almost all soldiers manning Jerusalem's three major checkpoints: Qalandia, Beit Jala Tunnel and Hizma. She had managed to sneak me in 'illegally' through one of them the night before. Huda's incredible sense of entitlement, love for adventure, and sense of humour meant that she was able in no time to alleviate my sense of apprehension. She managed to make crossing the Hizma checkpoint 'illegally' into a fun play. I put 'illegally' into inverted comas, as I do not see anything illegal about crossing into Arab Jerusalem. However as far as the Israeli authorities are concerned, every Palestinian living in the West Bank needs permission, a virtual one, as it is close to impossible to get one.

The day before, Huda had commanded me to meet her just a hundred metres before the checkpoint. I did. The second I got into her car, Huda's detailed checkpoint crossing instructions followed a series of warm and loud kisses:

'Suad put on your dark eyeglasses and get your cell phone out.' I obeyed instantly.

'Pretend to be speaking with someone, talk out loud and laugh all at the same time.' I was getting ready for the act when she added, 'Suad make sure to ignore those soldiers; never look at them or in their direction. Leave those bastards for me to handle.' Of course I did. We were finally first in a long line of cars waiting to cross the checkpoint, when Huda lit a cigarette. Knowing that Huda never smoked I knew this was part of the checkpoint play. Soon one of the soldiers waved his hand indicating that we come forward. While my heart skipped a beat or two, Huda acted coolly: she switched on a Lady Gaga CD to the maximum volume and preceded towards the soldier.

The combination of Lady Gaga's thunderous voice singing 'Born this Way', Huda's head and body rocking in all directions, and the fumes emanating from sequential cigarette puffs, made it look more like a hippie's car from the 1960s than a car 'illegally' sneaking in a writer to do her field work. *Zoom* we were weaved in. Needless to say, in a country where nothing makes sense only crazy acts do.

★ ★ ★

Nothing energises Huda more than a planned (or even better, a spontaneous) visit to an Arab house in what was once a majority Arab neighbourhood in West Jerusalem, especially if the visit is to her own family house, not far from Nahil's, in the elegant Greek Colony.

Hardly a week passes without Huda venturing on such a visit, either alone or with her mother, her son (when he was younger and she could drag him along), or any other willing family member. She often takes along friends, journalists or TV reporters. In fact she has been seen leading busloads of alternative tourists. Whenever she does this Huda runs the risk of having the Jewish family living in her house report her to the police, who come running to their 'rescue'.

Invariably, Huda's energy and excitement lead her companions to think that this is the very first time she has ventured to visit Arab homes and neighbourhoods in West Jerusalem. However, her facial expressions, neurotic energy, and the frequency of her nervous laughter indicate to the keen observer the deep exhaustion resulting from an addiction bordering on obsession.

Yes, obsession.

Like most Palestinians, Huda is haunted by the past and tortured by the unfairness of the present.

Nahil and I are with our guide on one of her many personally guided tours. These are not to be confused with the public tours organised by her organisation: the Centre for Jerusalem Studies. Huda's personally guided tours always cover the following topics:

1. Whose House is this One?
2. The Market Value of Your House Today
3. The Biggest Real Estate Theft in Recent History

4. Everything You Want to Know about the Family that Lives in Your House

5. Golda Slept Here

6. Nakba Survivors: A peaceful annual march to Arab neighbourhoods with the owners of these houses (whose ~~main organiser was Huda's friend Mona Halabi~~).

How I wish I could sneak into Jerusalem more frequently to go on all of Huda's tours. However this time I am on a specific mission: to meet, accompany and interview the protagonists of this book.

'Here is Mamillah Cemetery, this is where my grandfather, Jamal al-Imam, was buried. I don't know how much longer we can protect his bones and the bones of all the others before the Israelis bulldoze the whole cemetery. Their Jewish bones are sacred, but ours *al-zbaleh*, off to the rubbish heap,' Huda says from behind the wheel as she points with her right hand, almost hitting Nahil's nose.

I am sitting quietly in the back seat, and since my mission for the day is to deal with Jewish families living in Arab houses, I decide not to comment, to 'let the dead bury their dead', at least for now.

'Suad, see that beautiful three-arch building over there? That also belongs to Nahil's family. The Israelis are turning it into a five-star hotel.' I can hear Nahil sigh. I glance at the beautiful building from the rear window. I can easily imagine it as a luxury hotel. I want to ask if they know who the architect was (as I suspect, it turns out to be Andoni Baramki), but then decide it is not the right moment and keep quiet.

But soon the architect in me surfaces again.

I suddenly recall how, a few years ago, together with my

78

friend Rochelle Davis, I started to research an architectural book about Arab houses in West Jerusalem. I recall how empty I felt every time I stood to take a photo of those abandoned homes, now inhabited by Israeli families. It never took long for me to feel sad and walk away, while wondering who the owners were, what their story was, and in which exile they lived now. It was only then that I realised that what truly interested me in a building, a place, or a country were the stories that lay behind them, or in this case under them.

And that was perhaps when I also realised that the *hakawati*, the storyteller in me, was more forthcoming and had a stronger presence than the architect in me; a building remains a mere structure unless it has the ability to disclose a story.

Wanting to share a story about the YMCA building, I speak excitedly as we pass this peculiar neo-Byzantine stone building. 'You know, the YMCA building was designed by the same architect who did the Empire State Building, Arthur Loomis Harmon.' I get no reaction from Huda and Nahil. They couldn't care less.

I am looking out the window when Huda pointedly says, 'Suad, this was the Palestine Broadcasting building; this is where your Baba and Bayan's father, Ajaj Nuwayhid, worked. By the way, did you see the new film, *Huna Al Quds, Jerusalem Calling?*'

This gets my full attention. 'Unfortunately, I wasn't able to. I was away when they screened it in Ramallah. Friends who saw it told me I look like my Baba.'

'A carbon copy,' Huda says, laughing.

I giggle as I thought how some, like Umm Samir's daughter, tell me I look so much like my mother, and others, like

Huda, tell me I am a carbon copy of my father. My mother and father were not brother and sister!

I go back to trying to be the invisible presence on this trip.

While my eyes are busy skipping from one splendid villa to the next in the gorgeous neighbourhoods, it is easy to keep quiet. I am listening attentively to every word Huda and Nahil utter, though they are mostly Huda's. The one thing I thought I was sure of was that I did not want this trip to be about me, or about my parents who had lost their livelihood and their home.

But in a strange way it is about them.

I do not want to admit to myself or to any of the displaced Palestinians who appear in this book that, emotionally taxing as these visits and conversations are, to me they are therapy sessions. And as we all know, therapy sessions are often more painful than the pain they seek to alleviate.

The agonies and pain I feel as I accompany my protagonists make me realise that neither my body nor my soul are prepared to dig up my family's story in Jaffa.

I have buried deep the heavy burden of the past and the unbearable darkness enveloping the tragic events of 1948. Perhaps this explains my admiration for Huda's unwavering persistence.

Huda is actively incensed while I, like many others, plunge into silent gloom.

My reflections halt when Huda unexpectedly slams on the brakes. By the time I swing my head away from the window I had been gazing through she is already outside the car, pointing to the right. 'Nahil, Suad, look, look at this: Golda slept here!'

'Golda slept here!' I repeat, then ask, 'What do you mean, Golda slept here?'

'Golda Meir, right?' Nahil wants to make sure.

'Yes, *habibti*, Golda Meir lived in an Arab house.' Nahil and I peer out of the window. Huda continues. 'Nahil, *habibti*, I know how anxious you are to get to your own house, I promise this won't take long. Come on, you two, get out of the car.' Huda has parked in the middle of the road, her door wide open. She runs across the road and stands in front of a gorgeous three-storey villa. The size of the structure makes me think it must be a school, or a hotel.

'Now look at the ceramic tiles on the second-floor frieze, can you read?' Huda is in schoolteacher mode. I struggle to read the damaged navy-blue Arabic calligraphy on the white ceramic tiles.

'Villa Harun al-Rashid,' Nahil reads out loud. With her excellent Damascene Arabic she is able to decipher the defaced Arabic writing long before I could.

'Yes, Golda Meir lived in the Villa Harun al-Rashid in the 1960s. And when the UN Secretary General, Dag Hammarskjöld, came to visit "her" villa, she made sure to sandblast the Arabic script to conceal the fact that she, the prime minister of Israel, was living in an Arab house. And do you know whose villa this really is?' Huda never uses the past tense when it comes to Palestinian ownership of properties in Jerusalem or Israel.

The only person I can think of is Edward Said, as Talbiyah, where we are, is his neighbourhood.

'No, *habibti*, this is not Edward's house, but we'll soon pass by it and see the monstrous new building that's been built over the Said house. Villa Harun al-Rashid belongs to George Bisharat's family.'

Oh my God yes of course, this is the famous Harun

Al-Rashid Villa that belongs to my friend George Bisharat! Yes, yes it all comes to me now. Of course I read his article 'Talbiyah Days: At Villa Harun al-Rashid in Jerusalem' in the *Jerusalem Quarterly*.

Oh George this is so beautiful.

Asmahan dined here

Huda parks her car right across from the Aweidah compound. She makes sure to pay the parking fee for the anticipated one-hour stay. Considering the nature of our visit, it would be absolutely silly to be stopped by the police for a parking violation.

The mundane things one has to do in life!

Using the back alley, the two ladies cautiously enter the rundown garden of their huge compound. I follow.

Indeed, the compound is no longer used as a school, but somehow it looks more deserted than the active construction site that Huda had mentioned. Despite its desolation, or perhaps because of it, both of them, especially Nahil, look like intruders.

Their animated talk as well as their high energy levels give way to timid and nervous movements in no time. Even though this is Nahil's family compound I can sense that she is uncomfortable while walking through it: she is overly cautious and apprehensive, as if she were trespassing on someone else's property.

It is the occupation of the mind and the emotions that scares me most.

But this is Nahil's home, this is where she grew up, where she played with the other children in her neighbourhood, where she went to school. This is where she met her first love, and this is where her extended family lived.

As for Huda, this was her grandmother Aysheh's house. This is where Teta Aysheh lived before she got married and was 'demoted' by going to live with her in-laws in Jerusalem's Old City.

Huda's grandmother's tales about the rich life and splendour of this compound instigated her frequent visits. The obsession had started when she visited the house as a child for the very first time right after the 1967 war. Meanwhile Nahil, in the course of her sixty-three-year absence in Damascus, had nurtured her childhood and adolescent memories from afar. Like all other Palestinians living in exile since 1948, Nahil could not visit her house between 1948 and 1967. And since 1967, she needed one of those impossible to get permits to come visit.

While Huda feels very much at home, everything about Nahil conveys a strong sense of estrangement. Together, but also separately, they meander in what was once a lavish garden and through the narrow paths between the two houses. They stop here and there: touching this plant and staring at that stone. They poke their heads through this window and that.

I can easily imagine how high Nahil's adrenalin levels must have been in anticipation of a confrontation with an Israeli guard or any Israeli who might suddenly appear. I can imagine the fights and arguments between her family spirits and the spectres of the Israeli users of her property. They seem to be taking place inside her head. They probably also involve an argument with Amidar, the Israeli real estate agency.

Soon Nahil stands in front of a huge fig tree, places her palm on its cracked and coarse bark and slowly raises her head:

yes, she remembers. 'This must be the fig tree I would hide behind when I played hide-and-seek with my siblings and cousins,' she murmurs to herself.

Nahil continues her melancholic ramblings on a huge concrete slab for basketball which had been poured over the lavish garden that once separated the two identical houses from the main street. She looks up at the three suffocating Aleppo pines and feels herself suffocating too.

Having explored every nook and cranny at the back, in the gardens and all the narrow paths, Nahil finally joins me and Huda at the front entrance of her house.

The three of us stand in front of the two magnificent houses located on the busy Bethlehem Road (now Emek Refaim). My architect's eyes move quickly between the two identical houses. It does not take long for me to figure out that one is a mirror image of the other. The one to the left belongs to Nahil's father, and the one on the right to Huda's grandmother.

I can tell that the beautiful pink stone of the main elevations was brought from the famous *slayyeb* quarry of the neighbouring village of Beit Fajjar. *Slayyeb*, a very expensive stone, literally means hard and impermeable.

From the outside, I can see that both houses are typical examples of what architects call the liwan-house layout: one or two elongated living spaces in the middle with two or three rooms on each side – a total of six or eight spaces with a staircase to the side of the house.

The elevated one-floor houses have pitched roofs with red Marseilles tiles, also typical of the British Mandate. The most beautiful architectural details are the five huge arches of the front façades. Their bright white stones contrast beautifully with the pink, even eighty years after they were built. While the middle entrance arch is wide and flat, the two arches on either side are of the same height, but narrow and pointed.

Sadly, what were once very large glass windows overlooking a lavish front garden have become small windows with iron bars overlooking a huge expanse of concrete. And yet the Israelis claim they make the desert bloom. I keep the thought to myself as I look at the cement walls that block the five arches and at the huge cement slab.

Nahil and Huda's unexpected giggles interrupt my musings: they had left me to my endless architectural obsessions. I look in their direction. Huda is taking a series of photographs while Nahil holds an intriguing pose: standing on one leg while stretching the other over the slanting parapet that flanks the stairs leading to her house.

'As kids we loved sliding on this smooth stone parapet.' Nahil carefully balances herself as she smiles for the camera. I can see the mood has changed. Nice.

I pray that Nahil will not slide down that parapet. Her one-legged pose is dangerous enough for a woman of seventy-eight. But thankfully she seems to know the limits of her ageing body, and more critically our not being in a position to call upon the Star of David Ambulance were she, God forbid, to need it. For the Star of David would be more like a combat unit of Israeli soldiers arresting three life-threatening terrorists.

Once done with nostalgic acrobatics, Nahil carefully climbs the seven steps leading to the front veranda.

Nahil moves between the two windows flanking the main entrance. She presses her head against the iron bars of one window and then places her two hands around her face to shield her eyes against the glare. She is trying hard to peer inside her home.

Meanwhile Huda has gripped the handle of the main door, and, exerting all her strength and body weight, manages to turn it. To her surprise the heavy cast-iron door gives way. She looks at Nahil and smiles. Nahil does not reciprocate. She takes one step in the direction of the half-open door, looks inside the house and freezes.

Like a bronze statue she freezes. I have tears in my eyes.

The interior of the house is flooded with the light of the melancholic afternoon sun. Parts of what was once the living room liwan can now be seen. Huda slips her thin body through the gap between Nahil's bronze statue and the rusty cast-iron door. Nahil's stiff body quietly follows suit, and so do I.

There is silence.

Utter silence until Nahil's loud sobs echo through the whole house.

'See how beautiful these tiles are!' Huda attempts to break the awkwardness of the situation. They look at one another and smile. Huda comes close to her elder cousin and hugs her tightly.

'Yes,' she says, 'like everything else in this house, they are truly gorgeous.'

Silence prevails once more.

'Let me see if I can get some water to splash onto the tiles so that we can see their beautiful colours,' Huda says, stepping out of the house in search of water and escaping the throat-constricting situation.

Soon Nahil's eyes reflect that she is slipping into the past. I can now see that she is a child hopping around her house.

She runs to her bedroom and throws her school bag, and then her small body, onto the bed. She loves that bounce. Her sister Lamis is already at her desk, studying. Nahil resents Lamis's good study habits, which often result in their mother, Husniyeh, demanding similar behaviour of Nahil; while all Nahil wants to do is to run out of the house to play with the neighbourhood children.

Nahil leaves her sister in peace and follows her nose to the kitchen. The aroma of her favourite dish fills the house. She tiptoes closer to the stove and quietly lifts the heavy cover of the huge copper pot and noiselessly puts it aside. Not wanting to lose time or risk making a sound by opening the drawer to get a fork, she picks up a stuffed squash and a rolled grape vine leaf with her bare fingers. Before she manages to finish swallowing the burning hot squash, she hears her mother's reprimand. 'Nahil? Is that you in the kitchen? Please don't eat on your own, wait for your father. He's on his way home, soon we'll all have lunch together.' But Nahil knows better. Baba never comes home on time. He was always in his travel agency trying to satisfy his customers. So she keeps at it, grabbing another rolled vine leaf. *Mmmm, yummy*. She licks her fingers.

Nahil is soon caught red-handed, quite literally. She is cooling her burnt tongue with a cold glass of water when her mother steps into the kitchen.

'Stop it, Nahil! Please go to your room, or better, leave your sister alone. Go to your father's study and do your homework.'

'Why start now if Baba is on his way home?'

Both know that Adel will be late, but they still keep it up.

'*Habibti* Nahil, don't argue with me now, just go and do your homework.'

87

Nahil walks out of the kitchen, through the living room and out to the front balcony. She mounts the sloping stone parapet of the staircase and *zooooom*, slides down. She runs through the back garden just in time to see the train as it passes on its way from Jerusalem to Jaffa. Often, together with the neighbourhood kids, Nahil excitedly waits for the train to pass and flatten the nails they have just placed on the tracks. 'Heeeeey,' Nahil and her friends celebrate while their shrieks accompany the train as it travels between the two cities . . .

'Here, I managed to get you some water,' Huda announces as she pours it over the floor. 'Wow, look! Look how pretty they are, a bit like our tiles in the Greek Colony house.'

Nahil is still gobbling up her mother's yummy stuffed grape leaves. As the water splashes down, revealing the splendid colours and shapes of the living room tiles, her memory takes her on another flashback:

It was going to be the first time that Asmahan's mother visited them after the traumatic death of her daughter. Asmahan, the famous Lebanese singer who had just died in July 1944 in a suspicious car accident, and Nahil's mother, were good friends of the family. At the age of fourteen, Nahil shared in the havoc and hard work that preceded this famous visit.

Everyone in the compound is elegantly dressed, every single one: family members, women and men alike, and all the children; all the compound housemaids, the gardener, the driver, the cooks, and the waiters who have been hired for this special occasion. Like the two adjacent houses of her father and his brother, Nahil and her sister are dressed identically: two bright purple dresses with matching head ribbons and belts.

Every corner of the twin houses is scrubbed clean and in tiptop shape. 'Clean this corner just in case!' Nahil's mother Husniyeh keeps saying as she frantically goes around her house giving orders and bossing over everyone.

The big salon with the newly acquired Louis XVI furniture is kept open all day long. 'Kids, don't go in there.' Nahil's mother's instructions to stay away from the fancy furniture are repeated frequently that day. Like everyone around her, Nahil lends a hand. She carefully carries the silverware and helps in placing it on both sides of the blue and white china plates. 'No! Kids stay away from the main dining table, do not touch those crystal glasses, you can only help in preparing your table, the kids' table,' her mother keeps saying to her little nephews and nieces.

At fourteen, Nahil hopes she will be placed at the same table with the guest of honour, Asmahan's mother. If love of Asmahan's songs determined the seating arrangement, Nahil's place would be right next to Asmahan's mother. But Nahil knows better than to hope, even though she loves Asmahan much more than she loves Umm Kulthum, Asmahan's chief rival.

It is Teta Aysheh who announces that Asmahan's mother has arrived. In no time everyone is standing in their assigned places in the long welcoming queue: grandmother, aunts, uncles, grandfathers, even young cousins, everyone has a place. Nahil will never forget the elegant lady who walks in: tall and blonde, wearing a tight black dress, a long black fur stole and graceful high heels. No one in Jerusalem is as elegant as this Egyptian-Lebanese lady. She looks like a queen. The Queen is soon escorted to the sacred salon and the kids are instructed to disappear until lunch is served.

89

Nahil settles down next to her sister in the living room. They position themselves where they can see the Queen in the Louis XVI salon.

When lunch is announced they all follow the Queen and Teta Aysheh into the dining room. While waiting for everyone to be seated, Nahil is delighted to discover that the last two seats at the main table are for her and her older sister, Lamis. As she throws her body onto the dream-come-true chair, Nahil is instantly instructed by her mother to sit up straight, keep quiet and observe the rules of etiquette. With shaky hands she picks up the fork and knife and elegantly eats her stuffed squash and rolled stuffed grape leaves. Stealing continuous glances in the direction of Asmahan's mother, she swears to God that the stuffed grape leaves tasted much better when picked right out of the burning hot pot in her mother's kitchen.

Ending Asmahan's mother's visit to the house abruptly, Huda calls out, 'Nahil, Suad, let's get going. We need to get to our Greek Colony house before it gets dark.'

As we walk out of the compound Nahil approaches a window shutter. She leans forward and grabs a rusted cast-iron stopper in the shape of a woman's bust which was fixed into a stone windowsill.

'This is my bedroom,' Nahil pants, as she pulls and jiggles the woman's bust. She pulls as hard as her ageing muscles could. When she fails to get it out Huda tries, but the tenacious and rusty old woman refuses to leave home.

They leave her alone and walk away empty-handed.

On the Jerusalem–Jaffa railroad tracks

Soon the three of us are walking on the wooden pavement covering the old railroad tracks that once served as a never-ending playground for Nahil and her friends. Something about these tracks seems to have haunted the neighbourhood children and grown-ups alike. The power of the passing train, as well as its whistle and steam, provides a vivid image that they carried with them into Diaspora.

'It was on these railway tracks that Bayan, Mona and I spent the best days of our childhood,' Nahil says as the three of us walk along the narrow and endless path. 'We would place a few nails on the tracks and wait for the train to pass. When the driver saw us he would jokingly release the steam from a safe distance. Twisting and turning our bodies, we would laugh and giggle. But soon after, we would happily walk to our nearby school.'

I note that the little Jerusalemite girls placed nails, rather than coins, on the tracks; this makes me think that my mother's accusation of Jerusalemites being tight-fisted had some truth to it.

I am touched by the little girls' flirtations, especially when I realise that the Mona Nahil referred to is a friend of mine, and Bayan is the daughter of one of my father's friends.

This anchors me somehow and helps reduce the strong sense of estrangement that has accompanied me on this visit. Not that I ever feel at home when I venture into Israel. There is no other place on this earth where I feel such a strong sense of being a stranger than in my historic homeland.

Lost in Nahil and Huda's endless list of who owned what in this lost Arab neighbourhood, I gaze west in the direction of the infinite tracks and eventually find myself on the train, being carried from Jerusalem to my family home in Jaffa:

The journey from Jerusalem to Jaffa takes an hour or so. As I often do on trains, I watch the beautiful landscape go by. From Batir's bright lettuce-green plains to the dusty olive-green of Ein Karem's rocky valley. And once the scent of orange blossom reaches me I know it is time to stand up and get ready to get off the train. I stretch my legs as I wait for the train to come to a complete stop, and only then do I jump off the elevated carriage onto the narrow platform at Al Manshieh Station, our neighbourhood. And in less than five minutes I am home, having lunch on the terrace and looking out at the agitated Mediterranean Sea.

It is the very first time that I have gathered the courage to go back to my father's house on the seashores of Jaffa. It must be Huda's karma.

My daydream comes to an end when I hear Nahil whisper, 'Yes, yes, this is Mona and Bayan's house. Look, look at the Israeli family sitting around enjoying Bayan's balcony.'

5.

Whose House is This?

'HELLO THERE!' I YELL at the top of my voice, addressing a chubby, half-bald, middle-aged man standing on a second-floor balcony.

The garden, in the middle of which stands the two-storey house, is absolutely delightful. The old pine and cypress trees around the house, as well as the architectural style and details, make me think it must have been built sometime in the 1930s.

I may not be jealous of people with big luxurious houses but I am certainly envious, and in this case resentful, of people with such luxuriant, thriving gardens.

'Hi?' he answers back questioningly in an equally friendly and cordial manner. He walks around the table in the middle of the large balcony and comes closer to the balustrade. The two people sitting right behind him, a woman and a young girl, carry on chatting indifferently.

They are acting as if they were normal people in a normal country.

Huda, who is standing next to me, giggles, while Nahil stiffens.

The lightness and friendliness in my voice and his, as well as Huda's cheerfulness, make me realise what a spring-like day in November can do to people's spirits.

The luminous pink stone surface of the main façade of this gorgeous house reflects Jerusalem's splendid autumn light. As I stare at it, I feel as though it were reflecting the shade and shadows, as well as the bright and dark spots in my heart.

'Yes? How can I help you?' asks the balcony man as he leans forward across the balustrade in a welcoming gesture.

'Hi, how are you?' I greet him nervously once more, as if I had just encountered a lost cousin, not a lost house.

'What can I do for you?' the balcony man, perplexed, also repeats his question.

'We only want you to give back the house to its Arab owners,' whispers Huda, cracking her typical loud laugh.

'Shush, stop it Huda!' I nudge her with my elbow and swiftly turn my full attention to the balcony man. I do not want to lose this rare instance of a kind and accommodating Israeli.

'Do you live here?' What a dumb question, of course he does.

'Ye-e-e-s, why?' he answers, drawing out the vowel.

'I need to ask you something,' I say.

The balcony man is getting curious, as are the two others, probably his wife and young daughter. They too come closer to the edge of the balcony. The three exchange looks and a few words before the balcony man yells back. 'Coming!'

My heart skips a beat. Astounded, I ask, 'Did you hear what he said?'

'Don't worry, Suad, we can handle him,' Huda gives me a reassuring smile then adds, 'but let's act dumb.'

'In my case, no need to act.' I'm not sure I'm ready for this encounter.

'I can't possibly take this, not now and certainly not today,'

94

says an agitated Nahil as she walks away from us, heading back to her family compound. 'Sorry ladies.'

I am truly sorry to lose Nahil, the only one among us who grew up in this neighbourhood and who knows every single house and each and every owner, first-hand. But there is no time to mourn her sudden departure.

Since I have spontaneously and unintentionally (perhaps also irresponsibly) initiated this encounter with one of the many Israelis residing in Arab homes, I feel the need to be better prepared before we come face to face with this.

Desperate, I seek Huda's help. 'So, quickly, before he arrives, the downstairs belonged to Mona's grandfather, Adel Jaber, and the upstairs to Ajaj Nuwayhid, Bayan's father, right?'

Huda nods as the balcony man appears. My heart skips a beat.

'Hello, how can I help you?' he asks in a curious but polite manner – or as polite as an Israeli can be. He seems self-assured and happy. Of course, I too would be happy and smug if I were given a house like this.

Face to face with the balcony man, my anxiety vanishes. Up close he looks younger and less formidable. I am getting extremely uncomfortable and irritated by the normality and sweetness of the encounter, but Huda makes sure this normality doesn't last long.

'Whose house is this?' she asks, right up front.

Since I am intending to write about this encounter, I do not want it to end too quickly. I pose the same question in a less confrontational manner. 'Is this your house?' I ask.

'Yes,' he confirms, a bit bewildered.

'A lovely house and a most beautiful garden,' Huda says, a sly smile spreading over her not-so-innocent face.

'Yes . . . but the garden isn't mine. I live on the second floor,' meaning as far as the garden is concerned, he isn't guilty.

'Do you want to sell your house?' Huda is at him again. 'Because I am looking for a house for my . . .' But she is swiftly interrupted.

'No . . . no, of course not, why would I sell it?' he replies in an utterly dismissive manner.

'I am looking for an Arab house to buy or rent for my son, Mohammad.' I cannot help but giggle to hear Huda change her son's name from Hani to Mohammad.

The balcony man is obviously growing ill at ease talking to these not-so-innocent women, but he remains courteous.

'Isn't this the house of Adel Jaber?' Huda asks, keeping a straight face.

'I don't know,' he replies calmly.

'You don't know!'

As Huda gets angry he tries to modify his response. 'Well, not so long ago, some people from Canada . . .'

'From San Francisco.' I feel a strong urge to correct him even though it does not really matter whether Mona had come from Canada or San Francisco. I am also irritated by his use of the expression 'some people'. If the Israelis have been so indifferent, or even happy, as to throw 850,000 Palestinians from their homes, the least they can do is show some respect or a bit of sensitivity by knowing the names of the families in whose houses they are living.

As my anger mounts he continues. 'Some people came here a few years ago: they wanted to see the house where they lived before the War of Independence. I let them in, they took some photographs, and went away.'

End of story.

They went away when they should have stayed; they should have entered their homes and stayed there, I think to myself. His mentioning the War of Independence also gets to me. I have never understood why the Israelis call the 1948 Nakba, our Catastrophe, the War of Independence. Independence from whom? From the British, who helped them set up a Jewish state in historic Palestine? Or even more absurd, independence from us Palestinians?

While I am fuming, veteran Huda and the balcony man keep at it. 'Yes, I think it was a woman, but I don't remember her name,' he claims, or at best does not care to remember.

'Her name is Mona; she is a very close friend of ours.' Huda gets specific. Like me, the total denial is getting to her.

'But she told me it was not her house, she rented it from somebody.'

'And do you know who that body is?' Huda is gradually revealing her knowledge of every Arab house and every Arab owner.

'I don't know.'

'And would you care to know in whose house you and your family are living now?' Huda's tone is turning nasty.

'The owner of my house never lived in it.'

'So you got to know that he did not live in it, but you do not know his name?'

'No, I don't know his name.'

'Well, Sir, the owner of this building is Mr Hazboun, a very rich merchant from a very well-known Bethlehem family, and the tenant in whose house you are living right now is Mr Ajaj Nuwayhid. Professor Bayan, his daughter, happens to be a very good friend of ours. And do you have any idea who these people are?'

'No.'

I stand there and wonder if the balcony man truly does not know that Bayan's husband is the prominent PLO activist and intellectual, Shafiq al-Hout.

I cannot believe that he does not care to know the name of the owner or the tenant of 'his' house, the very house on whose balcony he and his family are now sitting and enjoying the cool autumn afternoon.

I stand there wondering about the total denial that underlies his lack of interest in who had lived there, who was kicked out from there, and who was prevented from going back. She came, took some photos and went away . . . end of story for him.

I wonder about his ability to not go there and continue to be in total denial.

In spite of my anger I am still curious about how he got to live in a house that was privately owned by the Hazboun family, who were never compensated for it. Contemplating the magnitude of the tragedy and the enormity of the absentee property and ownership laws which allowed a whole country to be stolen, I have no wish to continue to be personable with this relatively accommodating Israeli who stands there, willing to give and take (give only in words, of course). So I try to ask some more general questions.

'By the way, what happened to the property of the Palestinians? I mean the houses they own?' I, like Huda, purposely do not use the past tense. 'The houses in which they lived before 1948? Are they still under the control of the Israeli government or have they been privatised?'

'No, they're still with Amidar. They have sold some and are in the process of selling more, that is how I bought my house.'

I am getting extremely angry at his use of the expression 'my house'. Huda is also getting personal and emotionally charged.

'Oh yes, the infamous Amidar, which in 1997 sold our Greek Colony villa to Udi Kaplan, the Israeli real estate agency, when I could not get it back or even buy it just because I am Palestinian. He bought it, restored it, added an ugly triangular penthouse on top of it, and sold it for three and a half million dollars.'

'Three and a half million dollars, wow!' I can't help but repeat the price with a sigh.

'Yes, Suad, I am potentially a millionaire, all I need to do at this point is to convert to Judaism.'

'Why don't we all convert to Judaism? If a million Russians, half of whom were Greek Orthodox, migrated to Israel claiming they were Jewish, why shouldn't we be able to do the same?' I add to Huda's brilliant idea.

'It should be much easier, since half of us are already circumcised.' Huda breaks into hysterical laughter while the balcony man and I blush. Still, I can see that the balcony man finds the circumcision joke entertaining in an unsettling way.

'Yes, prices are going up all the time. Come on, ladies, be serious, all I can tell you at this point is, go talk to your lawyer . . . because it is very, very complicated.' The balcony man found it less painful to talk about property prices than circumcision.

'Bye,' he turns around and walks home.

'Bye,' we turn in the opposite direction and walk along the infinite train tracks.

And that is when I hear Huda mumbling to herself in an Israeli accent. 'Come on, ladies, be seghious, go talk to yough lawyegh, because it is all a very, very well-executed theft.'

That same afternoon.

Huda could have easily parked her navy blue Golf right next to her family house, but she does not.

Neither Nahil nor I notice that she has purposely parked it around the corner, further up the road from her house at 18 Uzia Street, as it is now called. 'I have no clue who Uzia is, or what Uzia means,' Huda replies dismissively when Nahil enquires.

Cunning Huda does not want to reveal the risks she is taking by visiting her family house. Her rooster-like walk and utter confidence make me feel relaxed and reassured. The normality of the situation leads me to believe that we are going to have a drink under the trees in their lush green garden, followed by dinner on their big terrace, exactly like the Jewish family we have just left sitting on Bayan's balcony.

'Here we are in the Greek Colony, see how charming and peaceful it all is,' Huda says as she locks her car. 'Come, let me show you around . . . You see that splendid villa? It belongs to the Greek family that sold Baba the land on which we built our house.'

I take note of the 'we' bit; Huda had not yet been born then. I do not want to dishearten her by pointing out that it is getting late and all that interests me, at this point, is to see the much-talked about villa of the Imam family. Needless to say, I am already emotionally drained from all we have experienced that afternoon. By now I know perfectly well why I rarely venture outside the safety of my home in Ramallah.

'Here it is,' Huda announces, pointing to a three-floor villa across the street from where we are standing. She has cleverly chosen the very best angle from which to appreciate the splendour of her family house.

'Wow,' I say, 'now I understand why you have been so fixated on your home. It's truly beautiful. Here, let me take a photo of you and your famous family house.'

'*Yalla* Suad, go ahead and do it quickly; Nahil, come closer.' Huda puts her arm around Nahil, acting like the older cousin and then adds, smiling at the thought, 'I'm sure the family will love to see the two cousins posing in front of the house.'

I am taking my time, trying to position them in the lower corner of the frame. I must admit I am more interested in the architecture of the house than in the two cousins and family nostalgia. Unlike Nahil's house, Huda's is in immaculate condition.

'Now I see what you mean by the biggest real estate theft.'

'*Yalla* Suad, *khalsina*, get it over with, take the bloody photo before we get into trouble.'

'Trouble!?!' I put down the camera.

'Why get into trouble?' Nahil asks, moving away from Huda.

'Oh well, I didn't want to alarm you, but now that Suad has seen the house and can write about it, I can tell you that I've been given a warning and threatened with deportation if I'm ever caught or seen in the vicinity of our house again.'

I cannot help but be alarmed by this important piece of information, however my admiration of Huda's courage and tenacity make me keep my fears to myself. I keep quiet.

'In the past, whenever one of the Blumberg family living in our house, especially Yo'av, saw me in the garden or around the house, they would all come out screaming and yelling at me. It all started in 1997, when Udi Kaplan, the developer, bought our house from Amidar. Soon after he divided it into two apartments, one on each floor, then added the monster I told you about on top.

'During the two-year period of renovation, I often passed by to check on the work. And whenever circumstances allowed, I would pick up an un-mounted window, a door, a piece of railing. You've seen them in my Sheikh Jarrah house, Suad.'

While Huda carries on dismantling her family house, I cannot help feeling uncomfortable about her violating one of the cardinal principles of conservation. 'Architectural details lose their historic significance once removed from their cultural context,' I say.

Exactly like the Palestinians who lost their significance once they were removed from their natural habitat, their homeland, I think to myself.

Huda is still at it. 'One day I entered our house and found the Israeli family that had just bought the ground floor of our villa from Kaplan. I had the satisfaction of telling them this was my family house. Meanwhile I started loading some of the floor tiles that the contractor had put aside to reuse into the trunk of my car.

'I could see that with the first load of tiles they were too stunned to react, but in the few minutes it took me to return for the second load they regained their sense of ownership and tried to stop me. All I remember was that Mrs Blumberg and I started screaming at one another, then shoving each other until we found ourselves on the floor. Her son, Yo'av, then ten or eleven years old, helped her up, while I was encouraged by the appearance of a sympathetic group of rabbis who had descended on me, no not from high heaven, but from the synagogue next door! *Et voilà*, since that day the house-war between the Blumberg family and me has never ceased.'

Nahil and I stand there listening attentively. Meanwhile I wonder what has happened to hurrying before we 'get into trouble'. Huda is taking her time telling us her epic saga.

'Now, whenever Yo'av spots me or my car he calls the police, then blocks my way with his father's car until they arrive. So now I've learnt to park far away so that I can run before the police arrive. Yo'av has become more efficient at it: he calls the police before he comes out to fight with me. As you see, with so much practice, we've both improved our war tactics.'

Both! Perhaps she has spoken too soon.

Only when Huda spots the police van from a distance do I understand what she meant by the Blumbergs becoming much more efficient.

'Oh, my God! Suad, run, slither away like a snake before the police discover that you sneaked into Jerusalem with no permit; the rest I can handle perfectly on my own, I'm used to it by now.'

With this sentence full of slithering, sneaking and snaking I am stunned for a few seconds, but I get my act together and swiftly turn away, instinctively and instantly taking a left and begin disappearing down a side alley. However, running for my life does not stop me from caring about frail, seventy-eight-year-old Nahil.

'What about Nahil?' I ask as I am leaving.

'Nahil has a permit, she's legal. Suad, for God's sake, just dissolve!'

I walk fast, then speed up, jog and finally run for all I am worth. Once I am at a safe distance I look back; no one is coming after me. I sigh with relief and slow down, allowing my heartbeat and adrenalin levels to stabilise. Huda's high-pitched voice, the angry tone of the police and the Blumbergs' screams all mingle with my late mother's voice. '*Susu, habibti,* escape is two-thirds of bravery, *il haribeh tultain il marajel.*'

Still, I cannot help feeling guilty and sad that I have missed out on the central scene of my book: when the police arrest Huda, handcuff her and push her into the back of their van.

While frail Nahil accompanies Huda to prison, I run all the way to Ramallah.

6.

Mother and Child

Jerusalem 1942

It was love and an unbreakable bond between mother
   and child
Her name was Aysheh
His name was Farid
She was born in 1891
He was born in 1909
She and everyone around her was ecstatic it was a boy
Soon after, she gave birth to three more
Fuad, Ni'mati, a little girl in a shadow, and baby Jamal
   who was in his mother's womb when his father died
Hence he carried his name: Jamal
Nevertheless Aysheh's first love was called Farid
Her second love was called Farid
And her third and fourth loves were Farid and Farid
Her last and only love was Farid
Farid, Farid and only Farid
Farid in Arabic literally means: rare, unique, nothing like
   him, the only one
'Not Aysheh but Umm Farid' she'd rather be called
   Mother of Farid
In 1930, Aysheh's husband Jamaleddine al-Imam died
She was then thirty-nine

And her beloved Farid was twenty-one
Together they cried as they placed the myrtle branches
    on his grave in Jerusalem's Mamillah Cemetery
She sat there sobbing refusing to move
Not because she loved him dearly
But because she resented going back without him to her
    in-laws
To the damp, dark and crowded house in Bab al-Silsleh
    in the Old City of Jerusalem
He helped his mother up, hugged her tightly, and made a
    vow:
'Mother, whatever it takes, you shall soon be back where
    you belong'
To the posh neighbourhoods outside the city walls
To a splendour similar to that of her own family: the
    Aweidah compound
Back to the German Colony where she, Aysheh
    Aweidah, a young and beautiful girl, had blossomed.

IT TOOK SOME TIME for him to realise his vow. Twelve
years later, in 1942, leaving everyone behind within the
city walls, Farid and his mother moved into their dream house
in the lush green neighbourhood of the Greek Colony. And,
as promised, just up the road from the much talked about
Aweidah compound. They proudly moved into their lovely
new villa, roamed from one grand room to another, from
one spacious salon to another, from one sunny balcony to the
next. They climbed up and down the oval stairs of their two-
storey villa with Asmahan's voice in the background, singing,
'Balashh tibousni fi 'enayyah . . . Do not kiss me in the eye,
for a kiss in the eye ends in separation.' Day and night, rain

or shine, Aysheh and Farid showed off their beautiful house, receiving family members and entertaining friends, inviting all to long and detailed house and garden tours.

Aysheh and Farid lived there happily.

But not for ever after.

Like everyone around them, on 20 May 1948, under fire, bombardment and siege they had to rush out, leaving one of their *ménage à trois* behind.

They were never to set foot in their dream house again.

7.

Husband and Wife

1958

S HEIKH JARRAH NEIGHBOURHOOD, IN what had become
East Jerusalem.

It was a tormented relationship between husband and
   wife
An older man and a much younger woman
Convenient for him and his mother, prestigious for her
At the end it was neither
A marriage that never bonded
But nevertheless was fruitful
Five children, five *aitches*: Hani, Hania, Huda, Hadi and
   Haitham

Her name was Bakiza
His name was Farid
And by now we know
He was born in 1909
She was born in 1939

When they married
She was eighteen
He had just turned forty-eight

Yet another forty-eight
The insecurities that numbers gave him were countless
Hence he married the young and the beautiful
On their wedding day everyone pretended to be happy
Even Mama Aysheh danced that day

And meanwhile another house was being built – in East
  Jerusalem this time
The three of them: Aysheh, Farid and Bakiza moved in
  together
Ages: 70-48-18

The dynamics among the three should be left to the imagination; the wilder the imagination, the closer to reality. Perhaps the archetype of mother and daughter-in-law was born in Jerusalem. Bakiza was also crucified there.

8.

Jealousy Was Only to Be Expected

June 1967

As in all wars, each side thought it would win
One out of might and fear
And one out of naïvety and righteousness

L IKE MANY AROUND THEM, Aysheh and Farid thought the
Arabs would definitely win the 1967 war, meaning that
the nineteen-year separation between East and West Jerusalem
and from their dream house would soon come to an end: they
would be able to go back to the splendour of their neighbourhood and visit its many cherished places.

Meanwhile in their Sheikh Jarrah home in East Jerusalem it
was business as usual – nothing out of the ordinary. Farid was
in and out of his travel agency, busy cancelling reservations
but also guiding the few optimistic tourists who remained
around the Holy Land sites.

Teta Aysheh, as usual, was bossing everyone around. She
primarily bossed her daughter-in-law Bakiza, and then in
descending order her five grandchildren: Hani, Hania, our
Huda, Hadi and even the little toddler, Haitham.

'How can a mother with a family of five kids disappear from
the house once, and often twice, a day? And only God knows
where to!' Teta Aysheh repeated a variation of this sentence

every single day. If words ceased to have an effect then desperate measures would follow. 'Here, why don't you scrub the floor?' Teta Aysheh would shout, throwing a bucket full of water and soap on the living room floor or, to delay Bakiza even longer, on the rough stone tiles of the huge terrace.

So as not to get into trouble with her ageing and increasingly jealous husband, elegantly dressed and fully made-up Bakiza, though boiling on the inside, obeyed. Such jealousy and vindictive acts often delayed her outings but never prevented them. Still elegantly dressed, she would quickly mop up the water and swiftly run out the door, down the stairs and out of the gate before Teta Aysheh could think of another household chore.

In a conventional and narrow-minded town like Jerusalem, rumours and gossip were not favourable regarding young and beautiful Bakiza. With an often absent husband and a strict and increasingly jealous mother-in-law, Bakiza was constantly leaving the house in search of small adventures here and there before going back to a large and demanding family.

Just a day before the war started, and in anticipation of heavy fighting in their Sheikh Jarrah neighbourhood, all the children were to go and stay with their other Teta, Bakiza's mother, who lived a few kilometres north of Jerusalem in the town of Beit Hanina. Well-equipped with argumentative skills and stubbornness, five-year-old Huda managed to get the three elders, Mama, Baba, and Teta, to succumb to her wish to stay home with them.

That evening, like most summer evenings, Teta Aysheh sat on the big terrace overlooking Nablus Road. While the main street was buzzing nervously below, the five kids' usual skirmishes were reduced to Huda's solitary hyperactivity. It seemed that both Teta and Huda were missing the four other children.

While Bakiza was running between the kitchen and the balcony preparing a late summer dinner, Huda ran excitedly in and out displaying her new clothes, the white dress and matching shoes Mama had bought her for Eid al-Adha, the approaching Feast of the Sacrifice.

Huda was trying to see her reflection in the shiny white Clarks shoes, and she called out piercingly to her grandmother, 'Teta . . . Teta . . . Teta . . . See how shiny my new shoes are!' She then placed them on the table in front of her Teta.

'Never put shoes on dining tables!'

'But they're new, Teta!'

'I know they're new, but a shoe is a shoe.'

Huda instantly picked them up, hugging them close to her chest and looking at them lovingly. 'I'll go and put on my white and pink Eid dress and the matching socks and shoes.'

'For God's sake, Huda, no, not now!' Teta and Mama scolded simultaneously.

Perhaps this was the very first time that Huda was not in a position to manipulate her mother's and grandmother's conflicting opinions. More often than not she exploited their differences to do what she liked.

'Let us hope there will be two feasts soon: Eid al-Adha and the greater Eid of returning to our house in the Greek Colony.' Teta Aysheh stared fixedly for a few seconds and then fell to prayer: '*Ya Rab, ya Rab, ya Rab*. Please, please, please God.'

It was one of the rare times Huda heard Teta recite suras from the Quran. Teta was so strong, she never needed God.

Once done with her recitation, she happily announced, 'Soon you will see how beautiful our house in West Jerusalem is . . .'

Huda interrupted her. 'Yes, yes, Teta, I know, I know it by heart. "Nothing compares to the house Farid and I built next to my parents' compound: the Aweidah compound."' Huda mimicked her grandmother's words in a chanting tone and giggled.

Aysheh's grandchildren often repeated her exact words, giggling at the same time. They had heard their grandmother speak those words hundreds of times until they were sick and tired. Even three-year-old Haitham was starting to imitate Teta's refrain.

Like the other children, Huda made fun of Teta's romantic memories of her house, but she harboured a secret: the only reason she stayed behind with the adults was that she would be the very first of her siblings to see The House. She so much wanted to see the one thing that made her Baba sad, so sad that it even made him cry.

Having given up the idea of putting on her Eid costume Huda quietly settled down next to Aysheh. They were both waiting for Farid to appear with the latest war news, and for Bakiza to bring out the delicious cool summer dishes: yogurt with cucumbers, garlic and mint, white goat cheese, her famous *tabuleh*, the crunchy breaded *fattouch* salad, sliced tomatoes, sliced cucumbers, green and black olives, and lemon squash with mint and crushed ice – everything that quenches the thirst of a hot June evening.

As expected, Farid came late that night. 'It seems that both armies, the Jordanian and the Israeli, are ready for war. This evening Jordanian tanks were seen moving close to the Mandelbaum Gate.'

'Farid! You and I can go and live in our house in the Greek Colony again,' Teta said, smiling.

'Teta! I thought you were taking me to see the house! Are you leaving Mama and me behind? Are you and Baba going to live there alone?' There was nervous laughter in response to Huda's not-so-innocent remark.

'*Wilik*, you naughty little thing. Not a bad idea, though. My son and I go back to live in our house in the Greek Colony while you and your mother stay in this house. A fair division, I would say.' Teta leaned forward and tickled little Huda under her chin.

'Not a bad idea. I like that,' Bakiza replied, trying to take control of an uncertain world around her.

Feeling a bit nervous about the direction the conversation was heading, Farid lovingly interfered, addressing his wife this time. 'No, seriously, Bakiza, which house would you rather live in?'

It was one of the very few times that Farid had hugged his wife so affectionately in front of his mother and little daughter. He sighed as he let go of her. 'Soon we'll all be able to go to West Jerusalem to see our Greek Colony house. I wonder what has become of it. I wonder if the furniture is still there, if the garden is in good shape. I wonder who lives in it now. Is it possible that it was left empty all these years? Nineteen years is a long time. It's felt like nineteen decades.'

'Soon we'll find out . . . *Ya Rab*!' said his mother.

Once again little Huda rejoiced in her father's beaming smile and the sparkle that appeared in his eyes whenever his house was mentioned.

This time there was real hope.

Hope that they would be able to return to their house in West Jerusalem.

Hope for Bakiza, but also for her mother-in-law.

Each to finally be in her own kingdom!

9.

Photo Albums

7 June 1967

T HE RUMOURS WERE RIGHT.
  The war did indeed break out on the morning of 5 June. Israeli tanks conquered East Jerusalem in no time.

And Israeli soldiers were entering Palestinian homes even faster.

Farid stood in front of the fireplace and fed the flickering flames fragments of his past. No one understood, not even Farid himself, what was going on in his head to make him burn the photographs of all the important personages in his life. Having been an official guide for the Jordanian Royal Palace, he had many such photos.

His mother stood next to him, nervously imploring, 'But why? Tell me why? Weren't you the one who always said, "If, and only if, I could have saved my photo albums? The Israelis not only stole my dream house but also my photo albums. A man with no photos is a man with no memories, with no childhood, it always felt as if I was born at the age of thirty-eight." For God's sake Farid, stop this foolishness. They are not here to look at your photo albums.' She was trembling.

But Aysheh also understood her son's fears: Farid did not want to be associated with King Hussein of Jordan. He was terrified of being interrogated.

Her entreaties were in vain. One photo after the other, Farid's recent past was disappearing. It was not clear which was faster, the banging of the Israeli soldiers on the front door, or the consumption of the celebrities' photographs by the orange flames.

Celebrity Photographs:

Here he was with a beaming face posing next to His Majesty King Hussein.

Here was Farid standing next to Her Majesty Queen Dina, the king's first cousin and also his first wife.

These photos must have been taken sometime in the early 1950s.

Here he was standing tall next to Emperor Haile Selassie of Ethiopia. Compared to the emperor, Farid looked like a giant.

When it came to burning the photos of the gorgeous Queen Farah Diba, second wife of the Shah of Iran, Ali Mohammad Pahlavi, both Farid and the flames trembled, but sadly her beauty was also consumed.

Farid stared at his photo with President Habib Bourguiba of Tunisia who had visited Jerusalem just a few weeks earlier. During that visit Bourguiba had made his inflammatory state-ment: 'Israel should be recognised by all the Arab countries.' Even though this controversial remark had made headlines and sparked demonstrations across the Arab world, the photo-graph could be of great use today. Farid's shaking hands carefully placed Bourguiba's photo in the centre of the coffee table behind him.

While Zohrab was King Hussein's private photographer, Farid was the official guide to all His Majesty's celebrity guests, including Pope John Paul V, who was about to enter the fiery flames when Bakiza took Farid by the arm, begging him to stop. 'For God's sake, Farid, stop it, don't burn the Pope, it'll bring us bad luck.'

Being married into a prominent Muslim family in Jerusalem, Aysheh was not particularly amused at the idea of being protected by the Pope. Nevertheless, she also thought that burning his image would bring misfortune to the household.

At this point a shaken Huda intervened by running to her father, tugging at the tails of his white shirt, repeating her mother's words. 'Please, Baba, open the door before the crazy Israeli soldiers blow it apart.'

Eventually Farid submitted to his daughter's demands and also sought the Pope's blessings, placing his photo next to those of President Bourguiba, and heading for the door to open it for the screaming soldiers: '*Iftakh, iftakh!*' BANG . . . BANG '*Iftakh il bab!*'

'Stay put, keep still, do not move from the living room!' shouted their commander as the other three soldiers began searching every corner of the house: up to the roof, into the attic, the bedrooms, under the beds, in the cupboards, behind the curtains, into Farid's study, out onto the balcony and soon into the kitchen.

Not finding the phantoms they feared, the soldiers relaxed a little. One picked up an apple and started munching on it. He seemed to be hungry. Since they started the war as early as three o'clock in the morning it was not surprising that by noon they would all be hungry. So as not to make the Israeli army look undisciplined and feeble, the same soldier while still munching on his apple gave his orders in a commanding, sweet-apple voice, using his rifle to point at each one of them. 'All of you, get ready to leave the house: you, you, you and you.'

The soldier's last 'you' landed on grandmother Aysheh.

The man had no idea of the trouble he had just got himself into. 'You, you, you and YOU!' Teta Aysheh yelled back at the soldier, stretching her right arm full-length as well as her index finger to point at each soldier in turn. With so much anger, Grandmother's extended arm looked much more threatening than the soldiers' machine guns. Nevertheless, her facial expressions and her twisted thick lips were so comical that she succeeded in uniting the enemies in nervous laughter.

In the tirade that followed she voiced her *arghs*, mocking the way the young soldier rolled his 'r's, typical of most Israelis.

She relished her role as the fearless elderly woman. '*Ya wlad il* . . . sons of . . .' but stopped herself from saying 'bitches' or calling them 'bastards'. 'Listen, you boys. In 1948 you took my house in the Greek Colony and my parents' house in Upper Baq'a and now, nineteen years later, you come again telling us to leave our house in East Jerusalem! Why don't you go back to wherever you came from! Go back to Russia, to Poland, to New York, Hungary or wherever. For God's sake, just leave us alone!' Her voice broke at this point. Looking at Farid for assurance she added, 'We are not leaving.'

Then, just in case she had not made herself clear, she corrected herself. 'I am not leaving my house, do you hear me, little mouse? Do you have any idea how old I am? I am eighty years old. Do you hear me? Eight zero. I am older than your grandmother. I shall not leave my house ever again, and will not allow you to take it, no, not over my dead body. Never!'

She then curled up on the pink sofa and wept.

Her daughter-in-law took note of the three extra years

Teta Aysheh had added to her age. Until the very last day of Teta's life, Bakiza would tease her, 'It took an Israeli army commander to make you admit your real age.'

'Get ready to leave.' The commanding officer repeated his firm orders. Coming closer to the pink sofa where Farid stood tall to protect his mother, he addressed him man to man and face to face this time. 'She can stay behind if she wants, but the three of you have to come down with me. Follow me.'

'Down where?' inquired Farid. He didn't know what to make of the commander's order. Did it mean that they would return home soon? But what if they didn't? Wasn't that what happened in 1948? He recalled all the horror stories of people leaving an elderly person or a child behind, thinking they would be back in an hour or so. One story after another echoed in Farid's ears. The images of the 1948 Nakba in which tens of thousands of Palestinians were forced out of their homes were still vivid in his mind. It felt as if it had all happened yesterday. Wasn't 1948 only yesterday?

'No way, I will not leave my house,' Teta repeated adamantly. And when Teta Aysheh said something more than once everyone in her family understood. It was final. Teta would stay behind.

Farid also knew that when an Israeli army commander gave a military order, that too was final.

Huda rushed to her bedroom mumbling, 'I will never leave . . . I will never leave. Get ready to leave the house . . . Get ready to leave the house.' She believed it was the end. Having heard over and over again the stories told and retold by her Baba and Teta Aysheh about their last hours in the Greek Colony house, and also about what had happened to the little boys and girls in the nearby village of Deir Yasin,

Huda knew that they were all going to die. But one thing was for sure: she was not going to leave behind her shiny new white Clarks shoes, or the matching pink and white dress.

She would go in style.

How appropriate for Eid al-Adha, the Feast of the Sacrifice, she thought. Her schoolteacher had explained the story behind this feast: it celebrated the time when the Prophet Ibrahim was going to sacrifice his son Ishmael.

From that day on, Huda had been ready to be sacrificed in style.

Just before leaving her room, after a final check in the mirror, her eyes fell on the photos of her three brothers and sister: Hani, Hania, Hadi and cute little Haitham. Only then did she realise how much she had missed them. Only then did she realise how lucky they were not to be dragged out into the street to meet their end.

She was reaching for the framed pictures when she heard her mother's anxious call. 'Huda! Huda! Where are you?'

'Coming!' Composed, she called back. But that did not stop her from climbing onto a chair and reaching the high shelf where the photo frames stood. She held each of them close to her face, stared at them for a while, hugged them close to her chest, before giving them long and loud kisses: *mua, mua, mua, mua*, one by one.

Did Huda cry? No.

'Bye Hania, bye Hani, bye Hadi and bye *habibi* Haitham.' She put the framed photos back and waved her little hand.

'Huda *habibti*, why did you put on your Eid clothes?' her mother asked, standing in the doorway.

'I want to die in my best clothes.'

'Oh, *habibti*, no one is going to die.' Bakiza hugged little

Huda tightly and wept. Even the soldiers standing there real-ised that Bakiza's tears and sorrow had nothing to do with having to leave her mother-in-law behind.

The four Israeli soldiers escorted Farid, Bakiza and Huda down the staircase into the garden, and then out onto Nablus Road.

Huda looked around her and saw hordes of people gath-ered in the street: men, women, children, the very old, the very young, and every age in between. Still preoccupied with her make-believe death-squad scenario, Huda was surprised that no one seemed to be properly dressed for the occasion. Some were even in their pyjamas.

Her heart skipped a beat when she saw a very deep and extremely long and undulating ditch in the middle of the wide sidewalk where she and her street mates usually played hopscotch. She wondered what all these people were doing in this tightly packed ditch that made her think of a long sardine tin.

She wondered when the Israelis had had time to do the digging. They must have dug it during the first hours of the war when she and her family were all hiding under the dining table. She had been unable to hear the noise of the digging in the midst of so much shooting and bombing, and the screech-ing of fighter planes flying over their heads.

When and where did the Israeli soldiers find such a huge number of Arab men, women and children? All of them, like naughty school children, had their hands held over their heads. This must be the death ditch, she thought. It all made sense now.

Some were silent.

Some were weeping.

Some were moaning.

Some were asked to speak up.

Some were asked to shut the fuck up.

Some were scared.

Some were resigned.

Some were told to sit.

Some were told to stand.

~~Some like Huda believed they were about to face their~~ God.

Meanwhile, the four soldiers escorted Huda and her parents here, led them there, walked them up the road next to the deep ditch, walked them back along the same sidewalk and then alongside the long death ditch. The ditch was packed, there was not a single space left to fill.

So much for Israeli military planning and for their calculations of the number of Jerusalemite Arab residents whose land they had just occupied. They got rid of the Arabs in West Jerusalem only to find them once again in East Jerusalem.

Tired of their heavy human burden, the Israeli soldiers released Farid, Bakiza and Huda.

'Just go back home,' yelled the same Israeli commander with the self-confidence all military people pretend to have.

Huda could not believe her luck: not only did her Eid outfit survive, but her parents had survived as well. Released, the three of them ran back home like bullets to Teta and the safety of their own home. As they were about to disappear behind the door, one of the soldiers fired a stream of bullets in their direction. The glass windows of the front veranda shattered.

'Because of those unexpected bullets and that unjustified aggressive behaviour, I never trusted the Israelis ever again,' Huda confesses to me forty-four years later, as she and I drink tea in the same house, in the same living room, on the same pink sofa where Teta had sat, anxiously waiting for them to return.

10.

The Visit

Three weeks after the 1967 war

Baba always kept a promise
But this time he did not
Every time I asked him, why not? He replied:
Whenever Teta Aysheh is ready we shall go
And when I repeatedly begged Teta to get ready she said:
Whenever Farid is ready we shall go
For weeks I was a pendulum between the two
And when I probed Mama to intervene she said
    indifferently:
Whenever Farid and Mama Aysheh are ready we shall
    go.

Whenever Baba was smartly dressed I would say:
Now that you're ready why don't we go?

And whenever Teta was elegantly dressed I would beg
    her:
Teta, didn't you always promise to take me to your
    house the minute they open East to West?

Teta often kept quiet, then sighed and moaned, Akhhh,
    ya Teta, akhhh . . .

T HIS WENT ON FOR weeks. Until Uncle Hassan, Baba's best friend, showed up early one afternoon to proclaim, '*Yalla*, come on everyone, get ready, we are going to visit your house in West Jerusalem.'

Wow, at last! I was in seventh heaven. I jumped up and clapped my hands and ran around the living room twice before disappearing into my bedroom. I slipped into my Eid al-Adha clothes and in no time was all dressed up in my pink and white dress and my Clarks shoes, excited and ready to go.

But when I stepped into the living room, Oh God! Teta and Baba were not yet ready: they were sitting on the pink sofa staring at one another. Uncle Hassan was sitting on the edge of his seat opposite them. 'Listen to me, Farid, listen to me, Aunt Aysheh: you will never ever be psychologically ready for this visit.'

It was the very first time I had heard the expression 'psychologically ready'. However, I have put it to great use and abuse ever since.

Teta and Baba gazed into each other's eyes for a long, long time.

Then when Baba looked away, Teta cried.

And I intervened. 'Teta, didn't you always say it will be the biggest Eid feast when we go back to our house in West Jerusalem? So why are you crying?'

Little did I understand.

We were not going back to live in our dream house in West Jerusalem, we were only going to visit it.

And how does one visit one's own house? I did not understand then.

And I do not understand now.

It did not make sense to me then.

And it does not make sense to me now.

And ever since that first visit, nothing around me made
sense again.

From East to West

It was Teta who insisted we walk to our house; the distance
between our two houses was a thirty or forty minute walk,
she claimed.

So when Uncle Hassan suggested we go by car, Teta vehe-
mently objected. 'Do you have any idea what has become of
West Jerusalem in the last nineteen years? It would be much
safer if we went on foot.'

Baba seemed convinced. Uncle Hassan realised it was not
the right moment to argue with a nervous wreck like Teta. I
had no clue why a happy occasion like this was causing so
much tension. A long-held dream was about to be fulfilled,
why so much fear and apprehension?

Once the difficult decisions were made everyone felt ener-
gised. Soon we were all trotting in disorderly rows on the
narrow sidewalk.

Teta and Baba in the first row with Uncle Hassan.

Hani and Hania, whose teenage energy made them flit
back and forth, left, right and centre, were also ahead of us.

While my little brother Hadi and I were hostages to Mama's
tight fists.

I was eight. Hadi was seven.

I later thanked God that our three-year-old toddler,
Haitham, was left behind.

The trip between our two houses took many turns and as
many ups and downs. Down the hill from Sheikh Jarrah, up the
road to the Musrara neighbourhood and then through an

empty space full of debris, rubble, broken fences and barbed wire. That was when the first words were uttered. 'We have just entered West Jerusalem,' Baba's trembling voice announced.

We fell back into silence.

For one reason or another Baba's announcement made me joyful, very joyful: at last we are in West Jerusalem, the paradise that Teta, Baba and everyone around me had gone on about for as long as I could remember.

'Nothing is as beautiful as West Jerusalem.'

'Nothing is as splendid as our house in the lush green neighbourhood of the Greek Colony.'

'Nothing is as stunning as 1948 Palestine.' And finally I was in the 'lost paradise'.

I was trying to absorb everything around me: houses with red-tiled roofs, apartment buildings, tall cypress and pine trees, cars, signs in a language I did not comprehend, white and blue flags on top of buildings, small shops, and the Yahud, the Jews. As much as my parents and their friends talked about the Yahud, I had never seen one before, except for the four soldiers who came to our house three weeks earlier: exactly on 7 June. And they were horrible.

I tightened my hold on Mama's fist.

I stared at every person who passed by: some were dark, some were brown, some were fair and some were as blond as Aunty Liz from London. The thing that drew my attention the most was the teenage boys and girls who were the same age as Hani and Hania. Unlike us they were shabbily dressed: they all wore shorts, T-shirts and sandals. I had no idea why, but for days on end all Hani and Hania talked about were the Israeli sandals.

Everything seemed under control until we entered an old

'black and white' neighbourhood. It felt like all those old films I never liked, except for the Charlie Chaplin ones that made me laugh. But this film frightened me; it made me tremble from the inside. I pushed against Mama's warm body, my two hands clutching her arm tightly. 'Stop it, *habibti* Huda, there's nothing to be scared of. These are normal people like you and I,' but her tone was neither convinced nor convincing.

'But Mama, why is everyone and everything in this neighbourhood in black and white? Can't someone do a colour tint for them, frame by frame, as you once explained they did with old black and white films?' Mama's giggles relaxed me a little, but not enough. Looking at the black and white people made me sweat. Though it was late June, huge men were dressed in winter clothes. Some even wore big round fur hats. I thought my eyes were playing tricks on me, like when I stared at the sun.

Everything around me was black, black and more black: long black frocks and coats, black shoes, black knee-socks, black shorts or trousers, black hats, long black beards, black hair shaved around the neck, long black side locks, and black cords dangling from both sides of their waists. I had no idea what these were for and didn't dare ask. The only things that were not black were the long-sleeved white shirts. Even boys my age wore black suits, black hats and long-sleeved white shirts.

Old and young women alike wore black. Not attractive black dresses: long black skirts, thick black stockings, black shawls and black head coverings, scarves and strange hair. And since the only time I had seen Teta, Mama and my three aunts wear completely black outfits was when Uncle Adel died, I asked, 'Mama, who are they mourning?'

'No one,' Mama replied dismissively.

A little way ahead I saw four boys my age. They came

running from a narrow side alley. They were the exact opposite, the negative, of the boys in black. They had light beige knee-length coats, same length robes, white belts wrapped around the open coats, white knee-socks and white conical hats. Everything they wore was beige or white, except for the black shoes. They too had their blond hair shaved around the neck with long blond side curls.

Unlike everything that Teta and Baba had told us all these years, West Jerusalem was very shabby and poor. There were clothes-lines with black and white laundry strung across the streets as well as over the public squares. Unlike our big and beautiful Sheikh Jarrah pink stone houses, those in this black and white neighbourhood were small, untidy and built of dirty grey concrete. I was so perplexed that I asked, 'Mama, is this a Palestinian refugee camp?'

'No.'

With such a definite no for an answer I had to figure out things all by myself. I kept dragging my feet in the narrow, unattractive and crowded streets of West Jerusalem. Oh, how much I wished that Teta and Baba would give up the idea of going back to our house in the West. I so wanted to return to our safe street and to our lovely house and garden in our beautiful East Jerusalem.

I also had no idea why these black and white people had put up so many huge black and white newspapers on their walls. I had never seen such large newspapers in such strange letters. Even Baba couldn't read them. Finally we came to a big sign that had one sentence in big red English letters. I was so delighted to finally see some colour and familiar letters, which my brother Hani read out loud: 'PLEASE DO NOT PASS THROUGH OUR NEIGHBOURHOOD IN IMMODEST CLOTHES.'

I automatically pulled down my pink and white dress – just in case.

All the men who stood next to the bulletin boards reading those enormous posters were wearing eyeglasses with thick lenses. I noticed that even little boys and girls in this area wore thick eyeglasses.

At that point, I recalled (but kept to myself) what our schoolteacher, Miss Leila, had once explained. 'Boys and girls who play with themselves end up wearing thick eyeglasses.' I still remember how we cracked up laughing at poor Salma, our classmate with thick eyeglasses, and how much Salma cried that day. I also remember that the next day both Miss Leila and Salma disappeared from our school forever.

It wasn't until much later that I realised we were in the Jewish neighbourhood of Mea She'arim, where all the Orthodox Haredim lived.

Once out of that neighbourhood there was colour everywhere in West Jerusalem. With the colourful background, Teta and Baba became animated.

Everything was familiar to them; I could hardly keep up or remember who lived where, whose office that was, and who owned what. They were pointing here, there and everywhere:

'Here's Jaffa Street; here is where we did our shopping.'

'Look, look, look! Here's the post office building. See those two beautiful buildings over there? One belonged to my father and the other belonged to Uncle Adel.'

'Here is Cinema Edison, this is where Umm Kulthum and Asmahan sang.'

'Look over there, that's the tower of the YMCA where I used to swim.'

'Opposite is the famous King David Hotel, we'll pass by them soon.'

Unlike the black and white Mea She'arim quarter, everything around us was nice and pretty.

Ya Allah, shoo hilweh inti ya falasteen! Oh God, Palestine, you are so beautiful!

I kept the thought to myself.

Everything was delightful and fun until we got to Mamillah Cemetery. Ah, I suddenly remembered, this is where Jiddo Grandpa Jamal is buried. The minute we walked into the cemetery Teta took the lead. She seemed so familiar with all those scary graves. Both Teta and Baba knew everyone's name and everybody's family in this rundown cemetery:

'Here is Ibrahim Hindiyeh, *Alla yerhamu*, may God have mercy on his soul.'

'Here is Said Dajani, *Alla yerhamu*, may God have mercy on his soul.'

'Here is his wife, Nahid Dajani, *Alla yerhamha*, may God have mercy on her soul.'

'Here is Abu Khaled Nashashibi, *Allah yerhamu*, may God have mercy on his soul.'

'Here is Siham Husseini, *Alla yerhamha*, may God have mercy on her soul.'

There were so many dead people in this cemetery it felt as if Teta and Baba had left behind more dead relatives and friends than were still alive.

Teta seemed to be composed till we got to Grandpa's grave. Her words were soon drowned by sobs. 'Jamal, I am so sorry we left you all alone for so long.' She knelt down on Jiddo's dusty grave and wept loudly. Soon we were all crying in various degrees. Once done reading al Fatiha, Baba leaned against his mama, hugging her tightly.

They seemed to be in a world of their own.

11.

A Dream House

O H GOD, TETA WAS absolutely right.
Oh God, Baba was also absolutely right.

Oh God, our house in West Jerusalem is absolutely gorgeous.

And every single thing that Teta had told us over all those years was also true. Our house in West Jerusalem was by far more beautiful than the one in East Jerusalem. The eight of us huddled close to one another. We seemed to be strangers in familiar surroundings.

We stood at an angle on the sidewalk across the street from our house.

'Stand still and don't move!' Baba nervously instructed Hani and Hania, who were too excited to keep still. Like all of us, they so much wanted to cross the street and enter our house which stood in the midst of a lush green garden.

Like Baba and Teta, we all stood across the street and stared at the house. We stood still, so awestruck it felt as if we were visiting a holy shrine.

'See how beautiful,' Baba eventually spoke. He was addressing Mama this time.

'Gorgeous,' replied Mama.

I could see Teta's eyes twinkling, I could see she wanted to say, 'See Bakiza, I told you so.' Instead she kept quiet, very quiet.

Baba carried on. 'See how beautiful the three-arch entrance is! Look how intricate the carvings are on the Corinthian capitals. It was on this veranda that Teta and I had our morning coffee every day.'

The Imam House
Greek Colony, West Jerusalem, circa 1985
Courtesy of Huda al-Imam

He gave Teta a warm hug.

I could hardly see the three stone arches Baba was talking about, partly because I was a tiny eight-year-old girl who did not want to ruin her shiny Clarks shoes by standing on her toes, and partly because the three arches and the carvings were hidden behind the trees: the palm, the pomegranate and the lemon trees that Baba had talked about so much.

'And look how beautiful that stone balustrade on the second floor is. That was where we had dinner every summer evening.' Like the Corinthian capitals, I had no clue what a stone balustrade was but kept quiet. Baba continued. 'See the green shutters on the ground floor? That is where my study and library were. And you see the shutters upstairs? On the left was Teta's bedroom and on the right was mine. The big kitchen and veranda were on the other side, in the back. The big salon with the lovely colourful tiles was on the ground floor, the living room with the nice Persian carpets was on the first floor.'

I was not sure why Baba was giving us all this explanation while we stood outside the house so I said, 'Baba, let's go see the inside.'

'Wait, *habibti*, wait, we have to see how they'll react.'

Before I had a chance to ask Baba who 'they' were and what he meant by 'react' he was crossing the street, moving cautiously towards his house. Like an excited herd we all followed him: Hani, Hania, Teta, Uncle Hassan, Mama, Hadi and I.

The second, or even before Baba could take hold of the metal handle to open the cast-iron gate to the garden, a dog barked, and soon after a woman in a blue dress appeared at the front door, right behind the three stone arches that Baba had been talking about.

She took a few steps forward and stood at the top of the five steps that separated her balcony level from the lower garden level where Baba stood. '*Ken, toda raba*, yes, good day.'

'*Toda raba*,' Baba answered, then switched to English. 'I am Farid al-Imam, the owner of this house, and I would like to show it to my wife and family, my mother who . . .'

Before Baba could finish his sentence, all hell broke loose. There was shrieking and squeaking . . . a rapid-fire barrage of Hebrew, Arabic and English words and short phrases.

'*Bagha! Bagha! Bagha! Leish inta houn? Bagha! Bagha!*' Out! Out! Out! Why are you here? Out! Out! 'What the hell are you doing here?' She switched from broken Arabic to broken English. 'Get out of here right away before I call the police! Sara! Sara!' She yelled at the top of her voice for her teenage daughter, who was by then standing right next to her.

'There's no need to call the police or make such a fuss, I simply want to show my wife and children our house,' Baba said as he pointed to us. I could see his arm and body were shaking. Uncle Hassan stood right next to him.

'No! You cannot show anybody anything! I say go away or I will call the police!' She turned to her daughter, 'Sara, Sara, call the police!' But the daughter remained frozen at her side.

Mother and daughter and the little dog resumed their screaming cacophony of broken Arabic, broken English, broken barking, broken Hebrew, then Polish (this I learnt from Baba later, though it also sounded broken to my ears).

Shouting back at the two women, Uncle Hassan protested, 'I don't understand why you are acting so hysterically, there is

136

no need for all this.' He put his arms around my frozen Baba as Mama and Teta pushed us back across the street.

The woman continued to scream. The daughter by her side also screamed. The frantic little dog stood right next to his master's feet and barked. He barked and barked, endlessly barked and barked, barked and snarled.

At that point we had no choice but to turn our backs and retreat down the hill.

For the whole of the forty-five minute walk back home all I could hear was the dog barking and the Jewish family growling.

And forty-five years later, I can still recall the little dog's hysterical barking.

Baba's rolling tears.

And Teta's unceasing sobs.

And it was on that day that I made a vow to keep visiting our house as long as I live, and as frequently as I can.

A constant reminder of whose house it is.

A vow that has since become an obsession.

An obsession that became as heavy as life itself.

12.

The Prison

July 2011

Huda did not sleep that night
But she may have dozed off
And since this was her first night ever in prison
This was only to be expected

She opened her right eye a sliver to look at her watch
It was missing
Only then did she recall what had happened to her the
   day before
She closed her eyes
And sighed

DAWN AND BREAKFAST ARRIVED together.
   She was keen on the first but could not be bothered
with the second. She could not tell which made her stomach
turn more, the stench of early morning eggs, or the exchange
of Hebrew and Arabic yelling between the prisoners and their
wardens. She did not know why there was such a commotion
to get up so early in the morning when they were to remain
locked up a whole day, a few weeks, a few months, a few
years or even a few lifetimes, like her neighbour Sharif, who
got several life sentences in prison.

This new perspective she had on Sharif's misfortune gave her the shivers, and her heart sank as she turned on the thin damp sponge they called a mattress. Untypically (these were unusual circumstances after all), like her Teta, she prayed to God: 'Ya Rab, ya Rab, ya Rab, please God, release me from prison soon.'

'Good morning, Huda. Inshallah, I hope you slept well last night.'

Oh God, who is that? Ah, Samira! She remembered her cellmate. 'My eyes never closed, not for one second,' Huda complained, stretching out both arms.

'Not true, I heard you snore and talk in your sleep,' Samira replied with a smile, leaning against the iron bars.

'Sleep-talk! You must be kidding! That can't be true.' At first Huda tried to deny the accusation but then quickly gave in. She knew about the sleep-talking already. 'What did I say? Tell me, what did I say?' Huda felt awkward about a possible embarrassment; she squatted apprehensively on her mattress to await the truth.

'Who is Hani?' Samira asked, then started laughing.

'Hey, don't let your imagination run wild. Hani is my son, al-hamdulilah balash fadaieh, thank God, no scandals,' Huda replied with a forced smile.

'You were also calling for or yelling at your mother,' Samira added.

'Yelling, most likely. Oh God, I thought I would get a break from Bakiza, my mother, at least for one night. It seems she accompanied me even to the police station.'

With a half-smile Samira added, 'Habibti, let me tell you, mothers never leave us, not even after they're dead. My mother passed away a few years ago and she still appears in all

140

my dreams. She's always scolding me, "Samira, I told you not this way! Everything you do or say is wrong, wrong, wrong!" I sometimes dream of her running after me with a raised slipper, trying to smack me – I often wake up in a sweat because of her.'

Oh my God! This woman must be well into her sixties and her mother still smacks her! Mine is an angel by comparison, Huda thought to herself.

It did not take long for Samira to forget her mother's flying slipper and turn her attention to her early morning breakfast. She peeled an egg, came up to Huda and offered it to her. 'Here, *habibti*, have this. You must be starving by now. You were so angry when you arrived here last night that you didn't touch your dinner. Here, eat this.'

Huda clutched at her stomach and turned her head away. She was about to throw up. 'I can't. My stomach is churning,' she managed to get the words out of compressed lips, then swallowed her saliva.

'OK.'

In no time Samira's mouth was full of egg. She ate hers first, then Huda's, one after the other, followed by a biscuit. She was now chewing away leisurely and rolling her tongue. The offensive chomping wouldn't end.

Huda finally had enough. She not so subtly covered her face with her hand to shield her nostrils against the smell. Once she was done munching her eggs, Samira again tried to tempt Huda into eating something. 'Try this. I tell you, their jams are delicious. Try this yummy apricot one. Believe me, these Jewish jams are even better than the ones I make at home. Goddamn, whatever they do, they do well, not like us Arabs.'

Huda did not agree with her cellmate on Jewish supremacy in jam-making, but she let it go. 'No, Samira. Please leave me alone, I can't eat anything.' Huda stretched out on the mattress, desperately turning her face to the wall.

'OK, OK, I see you're still upset, my dear Huda. Soon you'll get used to prison. Remember, we're all here because of our love for our country, not because we've committed a crime against them. They commit all sorts of crimes against us, then turn around and arrest us and throw us into prison. Remember, *habibti*, one-third of Palestinian men have been to Israeli prisons. Do you think they were all criminals?' She barely paused for breath before continuing. 'Umm Sabri, the cleaning woman who was here before you, was arrested because she sneaked into Israel without a work permit. Poor thing, she was even older than me. Her two sons are in prison, and imagine, she has to work at her age to feed nine grandchildren.'

Ignoring Huda's moans Samira carried on. 'And the young woman, Siham, the one who left yesterday before you arrived, she was from Ramallah, from a village near Ramallah, I forget the name, it could've been Bibwan, Beitunia, Betinia, something that starts with a "b". Anyway to cut a long story short, she came to visit her mother in the Al-Maqased Hospital and she was arrested because she didn't have the necessary permit to visit Jerusalem. Siham was like you; she cried day and night for a week until someone from her family eventually bailed her out. I tell you, we're a money-making machine for the Israelis and that's all there is to it. "Security" my ass.'

Huda, whose headache was getting worse as a result of Samira's incessant stream of stories, could not help but appreciate the 'security my ass'. 'If the security of a country means the annihilation of another nation then there must be something structurally wrong with that country,' she said in response.

Samira ignored Huda's intellectual remark and carried on recounting the stories of those who had passed through her prison cell. 'The one before Siham was from the town of Anata. They arrested her because she tied herself to one of her olive trees when Jewish settlers tried to burn it. She was lucky not to have been burnt along with her trees. Trust me, the settlers would do it. And the Silwani woman was imprisoned because she shoved the Israeli official who handed her the demolition order for her house. When the bulldozer arrived she refused to leave, so they carried her away and brought her to me.'

Huda was getting tired and terribly bored with all these depressing yet familiar stories. She realised how eager Samira was to have a listening ear, having spent so many months in prison not knowing when the next cellmate might arrive. With difficulty Huda finally managed to interrupt her torrent of stories. 'And you, Samira, how long have you been in prison to know about all these cases?'

'Four months. But this is my third time. And this time, excuse my language, *Sitt* Huda, it's the fucking Israeli *arnona* tax.'

Samira paused briefly. 'See, *habibti* Huda, don't be so sad. We're not criminals, we're all heroes and heroes need energy, so here, have something sweet.' Samira broke into a nervous laugh as she spread a large spoonful of orange marmalade on a tiny piece of bread. 'Here, Huda, try this marmalade, it's truly good. The only thing I'll miss if I ever make it out of this damn place is their damn good marmalades and jams.'

And then the chomping started all over again: *mtaa . . . mtaa . . . mtaa . . .*

At this point Huda pressed her right ear against the dirty mattress (which also smelled), her right palm still covering her nostrils, while her left palm pressed against her left ear. They must have placed her with Samira as part of her punishment. She found herself seriously considering quitting her repetitive visits to her father's house in West Jerusalem.

Huda felt that the only way she could end the saga of the morning egg stench and Samira's loud munching and licking of marmalade off her sticky fingers was by resuming their pre-breakfast conversation. Despite her great discomfort she sat up on her mattress. 'Once I'm done with the Israeli trial, hopefully soon, I'll have to go home and face another two harsh trials: one from my son, Hani, and another from my mother, Bakiza. They both get so mad at me whenever I visit my father's house in the Greek Colony, and I do it almost every week . . .'

Samira could not keep quiet any longer and interrupted, 'Sister, what use is it visiting your father's house in West Jerusalem? You see what happens to you when the Jewish family calls the police and complains, all it takes the Balloons family, or whatever their name is, is to make a . . .'

'The Blumbergs,' Huda corrected her.

Samira gave her a blank look before continuing. 'Whatever their name is, for the Jewish Balloon family it's only a matter of a phone call; but for you and your family it's a big head-ache. And look at you: a nice, elegant, respectable lady thrown into prison, and for what? Tell me, for what? We can hardly keep our houses in East Jerusalem, let alone West Jerusalem. Come on, forget your house in West Jerusalem, that's over with, *khalas*, enough, 1948 is history.'

At this Huda could not help but remember the Israeli officer who had interrogated her only a few weeks ago. 'Stop living in the past, that's your problem. You Arabs continue to live in the past,' he had lectured her with growing impatience. 'Wake up, it's 2011, not 1948. *Khalas*, Huda, *khalas*, it's all over,' he had shouted at her.

His words echoed in her ears. For a fraction of a second a terrible thought flashed across her mind: could it be that Samira was an *asfourah*, a bird, an informer? As far as Huda knew, no one was kept that long in the Russian Compound which functioned mostly as an interrogation centre rather than a long-term prison. But she quickly convinced herself and dismissed these paranoid suspicions regarding her innocent cellmate. She continued, 'My mama is truly terrified that if I keep visiting our house in the West and keep bugging the Blumbergs, the Israeli officials will ultimately punish me by throwing us out of our house in East Jerusalem. I mean not only me, but my son and my mother as well.'

'Your mother is certainly right on this one, Huda, you should know better. They've done that many times already: didn't they evict the Ghawi and Hannoun families from Sheikh Jarrah, your neighbourhood? Isn't that where you live? They also evicted the al-Kurd family from their house in Wadi al-Jouz. Poor Abu Kamel, he couldn't bear being thrown out, he ended up with a stroke that finished him off, right then and there. Look at his poor wife, Umm Kamel: she squatted in a tent next to her house, then what? Six months later, only God knows where they took her. The poor thing, she ended up with no husband and no house. Huda, listen to me, they won't rest till they get rid of all of us Arabs in East Jerusalem. So stop being silly, visiting your 1948 house in

Jewish Jerusalem. It's no use, believe me, no use. I'm surprised that an educated woman like you gets herself into so much trouble. Sorry, *habibti*, I don't understand why you go looking for trouble. Do you need more problems to add to the ones they create for us every single day?'

Huda kept quiet, thinking to herself: How can I explain to Samira the vow I made to myself to visit my father's house in West Jerusalem as often as I could, for as long as I live? The vow I made forty-five years ago, on 7 June 1967, when I saw Baba's tears rolling down his cheeks. How can I explain to Samira what an obsession is? How can I explain that one does not control an obsession, it's the other way round, it's the obsession that takes hold of you? Huda sensed that she was becoming obsessed with her obsession. How can I admit to a stranger, who may be an informer, how taxing and painful it has been to keep true to a vow? Oh, how I wish I could be indifferent! How I wish I could get away from it all, living in Amman, Beirut, Dubai, San Francisco or Australia like so many others, including my own sister and brothers.

But don't we carry all that baggage with us wherever we go? Was I making those visits for myself or for Baba? If for my own sake, then I'm tired of it all, and if for my late father's sake, then that's become a real burden: Baba, is it at all fair that you pass away thirty years ago and leave me with this weight to carry? Every day I ask myself, why am I doing this?

Has this become a vendetta between me and the Jewish family that lives in our house?

Between me and the police officer who keeps arresting me?

Whatever it is, and for whatever reason, I am so damn exhausted.

Huda broke down crying.

Or was it all the fault of that little dog that incessantly barked and snarled at us when we went to visit our house for the very first time? Huda thought of that nasty little dog and then smiled. 'Huda! For God's sake, why are you crying? You cry and smile all at the same time. Explain to me why you go there and get yourself into trouble?' Samira's question halted Huda's thoughts. It took her a while to remember what Samira's question was. Then she said, 'Listen to yourself, Samira; you and my mother and Hani are all harder on me than the Israelis themselves.'

'No, no, *habibti*, you're wrong on this one. There is no one on the face of this planet crueller to us than the bloody Israelis. Look what they've done to me. They . . .' Huda had already heard Samira's story, at great length and in minute detail, from the very minute the warden clicked open the iron door and pushed Huda into Samira's tiny sphere. But that did not stop her from repeating it for the third time in less than fifteen hours. Yet this third edition included some new facts.

'Listen to what the bastards, *il arsat*, excuse my language *Sitt* Huda, did to me. A week after I had settled with them and paid the thirty-five thousand shekels for the house *arnona*, they came back demanding I pay the television *arnona* for the last five years. They insisted that I had to pay another ten thousand shekels! After having paid every last penny I had and more for the house *arnona*, where would I get more money? You tell me. I told the officer, even if you try to sell me body and soul in the souq you will not get a thousand shekels.'

Huda couldn't help giggling as did Samira, without the slightest pause in her story.

'I told the damn Israeli officer who came to check on the contents of my house that it wasn't me but my brother Ali who bought the TV set. I didn't want a TV in the first place. Ali bought it then went to Detroit. He never sent me a single penny and now you want me to pay his TV tax! The officer said that if I didn't pay the tax they would take away the TV. Sure enough the bastard walked off with my TV on his hip, but not before he threatened to come back in two weeks if I didn't pay up. And sure enough, there he was on my doorstep two weeks later and this time he brought along two big men who carried away my fridge; a week later, my washing machine; then my living room furniture; then my bed and closet with all my clothes in it. Then, two months later when I still couldn't pay, they finally came and carried me away. And here I am in prison until Allah *yifrijah*, until I get released from jail and my troubles. How? Don't ask me.'

While Samira went on with her *arnona* saga it dawned on Huda that perhaps *arnona* was the word most frequently used by Palestinians in East Jerusalem. *Arnona* this and *arnona* that is all one hears in the streets, on buses, at home, work and even at demonstrations. Perhaps the Jerusalem *arnona* had become a main cause of 'the crazed of Jerusalem' syndrome.

Samira was still talking. 'Sometimes I take it easy on myself by swearing to God, *wallahi*, it's better for me to stay here in this cell. They do all the shopping for me; they do all the shopping, cooking and washing up for me, the only thing I miss is my mattress. I once joked with the Israeli officer, telling him that if they planned on keeping me here long enough they could at least give me back my good mattress. You know what the bastard replied? "Instead of us giving you back your mattress why don't you get your rich cousin Anis to bail you out?" *Fil mishmesh*, in your dreams. I tell you, Huda, with the service-free *arnona* they impose on us and the many fines and penalties we East Jerusalem Arabs pay them, we've become the casino where they always win . . . or even better, the cash cow that they continue to milk.'

Only when Samira stopped to take a deep breath did Huda notice that her eyes were brimming with tears. She couldn't tell whether Samira was laughing or weeping.

'*Sharu il baliyyat ma yudhek*,' Samira concluded before finally sinking into a deep silence. The worst disaster is that which makes you laugh. Slowly she slid against the iron bars behind her and squatted on the floor.

Huda looked closely at Samira's worn-out face and thought how young and fortunate she was by comparison. A whole city seemed sunk in the deep cracks of Samira's wrinkled face.

It made Huda think how fatigued her beloved city was. Made her think of all the worn-out Jerusalemite faces around her: her young son, Hani, her ageing mother, Bakiza, all her relatives, most of her friends, the neighbours, her colleagues at the university, certainly the students and every shop-keeper she knew, inside or outside the city walls where she lived and worked.

Every single person she knew in East Jerusalem had an ongoing exhausting saga with the Israelis. They were all trying hard to hang in there.

Like Samira, Huda started counting them and their problems, one by one:

Musa, whose family had always lived in Jerusalem, where he himself was born and raised and now, only because he had married Lisa, an Englishwoman, he had to fight the Israelis day and night to keep his Jerusalem residency.

Rema, and the agonising process of renewing her Jerusalem ID every single year.

Nurjihan, who could not have her Ramallah husband, Khaldun, live with her and their children in Jerusalem.

Two-year old Qaisar, who had been deprived of his Jerusalem ID because his mother was from Jerusalem while his father was from the West Bank.

Hidaya and Ribhi, who were forced to close a century-old business, the famed National Hotel, due to impossible debts and *arnona* problems.

Huda's own sister and three brothers who had lost their Jerusalem ID cards simply because they stayed abroad longer than two years.

All those whose houses had been demolished, the ones Samira had mentioned and more: the Ghawis, the Kurdis and the Hannouns, as well as the twenty-two Arab families living in Sheikh Jarrah who had been given eviction orders.

She thought of the city itself: the 'capital' that had lost all its Arab suburbs because of a monstrous concrete wall that had been built around it.

A city that had been isolated from its Arab surroundings, the West Bank and Gaza.

As the list got longer and longer Huda started wondering whether she, like Samira, would not mind spending a few weeks in prison, away from it all.

God, is this troubled place truly your Holy City?

At that very moment Huda's daydream (or nightmare) came to an end. She heard her name called by the prison warden. By the time he appeared and clicked open the iron door to their tiny cell, Huda, like an obedient soldier, had stood up to her full height.

'Huda.'

'Yes,' she replied promptly.

'Follow me.'

Wearily, Huda dragged her chained feet, and taking small steps came up close to Samira and kissed her on both cheeks. It felt like she had been Samira's mate for sixteen years rather than sixteen hours.

'Good luck, Huda. I know for a fact that you'll keep visiting your family house in West Jerusalem, but remember, it's far more important that you protect your Sheikh Jarrah house.'

Huda smiled.

Samira leaned against the shut iron door, waiting for the next delivery.

13.

The Iraqi Officer

'HUDA! ONE MORE VISIT and you'll be deported, do you understand what I'm saying?' he shouted at her in Hebrew.

She reminded him that she neither spoke nor understood Hebrew. He shifted to Arabic, her mother tongue and perhaps his as well.

'Huda! *Il marrah il jay ib'aad, mafhoum?*' he repeated in Arabic with an Iraqi accent.

He called her by her first name, Huda.

She argued back with familiarity and no inhibitions.

Stop going there.

Leave those people alone.

Leave them in peace.

Stop terrifying them.

The police officer formulated his statement in as many ways and forms as possible. 'You're terrorising them, do you realise that?' The more he explained the happier and more satisfied she felt.

'Do you have any idea what these people think or how they feel whenever you appear there?' He looked Huda straight in the eye.

'And how do they feel, Captain Ya'kov?' she answered

back, then cracked a mysterious Mona Lisa smile. 'And what do they think?'

'You are not allowed to appear on their doorstep anymore,' he snapped back. Anticipating and refusing to hear the response she often gave him, as they already had a long history of interrogations, he continued, 'Now you listen to me carefully. You are not to go there again. You are not to set foot on their doorstep. You are not to enter their garden.'

'I no longer tread on the doorstep nor do I enter the garden,' she almost parroted, making sure to use the article 'the' and not 'their'.

'Do I need to remind you that not so long ago you went into the garden and picked pomegranates?'

'Wouldn't you pick pomegranates off the tree your father planted?' She flashed him a big smile this time.

He stared at her shining brown eyes, saw her familiar mischievous smile, then assumed a pose not unlike Rodin's Thinker before saying wearily and yet firmly, 'In the past it was your father's house; today it is not.'

'Today it is not,' Huda mechanically repeated after him, then added, 'Why not?'

'Why not what?'

'Why is it no longer my father's house?' She hesitated before adding 'my'.

'Huda, I hope you realise that you are in the Moriaya Police Station, and more specifically, in prison,' he emphasised. 'You are not in the History Department at Al Quds University or at Mount Scopus.'

He broke into loud, self-satisfied laughter.

Wanting to ease the tension to her advantage, Huda pretended to join in the laughter.

'Huda, by now you should know that this is absentee property and that nothing has changed since I saw you last, which was less than a month ago.'

'Do I look like an absentee to you? Is it a crime for an absentee, or a ghost, to visit their father's garden? Are you arresting a ghost?'

'Your ghosts are worse than your real selves!' he retorted, rolling his eyes.

Considering the unbearable presence of her father's ghost, Huda completely agreed with the officer's comment. The presence of the absent could indeed be agonising.

Captain Ya'kov's patience was reaching its limit. 'Alright, enough!' His eyes opened wide. 'And stop living in the past. That is your problem. You Arabs continue to live in the past.'

'When it comes to Jews, you have a two-thousand-year memory, but when it comes to us Palestinians, you have a sixty-year amnesia.'

Even though dealing with Huda's obsession was much less dangerous than dealing with the many drug and criminal cases waiting for him downstairs, he did not want to spend any more time on the Imam's house.

Captain Ya'kov gave his final verdict yet again. 'Huda, next time we receive a phone call from Yo'av or any other member of the Blumberg family complaining about you being at their doorstep, or that you're in their garden picking lemons or pomegranates or in front of that house, or even across the street from it, I will throw you in prison, take you to court and prosecute until you're deported.'

As with all Palestinians, the word 'deport' chilled Huda to the bone.

Realising that he had finally taken control of the situation,

the officer repeated, 'Next time deportation, Huda. *Ib'aad*!'
he yelled in Arabic.

Terrified, Huda kept quiet.

Disconcerted by her unusual silence, Captain Ya'kov stood
up, went around his desk, came up to Huda and removed her
handcuffs.

Part Four
Elie: A Bird's-Eye View

14.

A Businessman from Tel Aviv

E LIE WAS SIPPING THE very last drops of his *digestif* when we walked into the trattoria.

He greeted us enthusiastically. '*Fantastiques, marveilleuse, délicieux.*' Why in French? First, because he had grown up in Lebanon and second, because he had been living in Paris since 1982.

Everything about Elie – his beaming face, flushed chubby cheeks, drooping eyelids, and most noticeably the huge serviette wrapped around his neck – indicated his indulgence in the too-many-course meal: *l'antipasto, il primo piatto, il secondo, il contorno, il dolce, il vino*, even *l'aqua minerale* Badoid.

Perhaps part of Elie's apparent satisfaction was also that he had managed to escape from our three-day conference and its intellectual indulgence on Palestine.

The four of us, the renowned Palestinian economist and writer Jamil Hilal, his Italian wife, Piera, a development specialist, Anna, an Italian journalist and I, eagerly followed the waitress who seated us in an alcove with only one table. The young waitress handed each one of us a menu and disappeared swiftly.

Unlike Elie, who had the time to enjoy his elaborate meal, we had to rush. In less than an hour we were to attend Elie's presentation on the late Palestinian poet Mahmoud Darwish. Once each of us had made our selections from a long list of mouth-watering possibilities, I hurried out of our hidden alcove in search of the waitress, lost among the buzzing tables of noisy customers.

I was more than happy to practise my Italian. I wanted to alert our waitress to the fact that we were in a hurry. To make sure I got it right I divided my request into two simple short sentences: first, 'we're in a hurry' and second, 'the four of us want to eat'. And since eating in a hurry is not exactly the norm in an Italian restaurant, I tried to emphasise the hurry part: '*Siamo in fritta*' and then '*Vogliamo quattro persone per mangiare*'.

The waitress, who had been very polite until then, said, 'You can start by eating me and my friend Francesca,' pointing to the waitress standing next to her. 'And I shall run and get you two more people to eat.' She then called out, 'Alberto *e* Alessandro *venite qui subito*,' come here quickly. I later learnt that I had said, 'We are being fried and we would like to eat four people.'

Soon, we were swallowing our truffle pasta and truffle gnocchi and the excellent *corposo* red wine recommended by Elie, who had in the meantime joined our table and asked the waitress for a wine glass. Knowing what a gourmet Elie was, I had made exactly the same choice of plates that he had ordered and so obviously enjoyed.

I had done the same thing the day before when I encountered Elie wandering in Bellinzona's food market – this at a time when he and I were supposed to be at the Teatro Sociale where the Babel literary festival events on Palestine were taking place.

I hope you understand why a Palestinian has no desire to attend anything Palestinian (or on Palestine), but opts instead for the food market. Elie was standing in front of a cheese stall tasting a dark red cheese, then a dark yellow one. After an elaborate process of cheese selecting, tasting and chewing, his facial expression, as well as the continuous nodding of his head, indicated Elie's full satisfaction. In addition to the red wine cheese and the yellow beer cheese, he sampled a third, and then a fourth.

I didn't find the idea of beer cheese or wine cheese particularly appealing, but having so much confidence in, and appreciation of, gourmets like Elie, I ended up buying whatever he bought.

With a mother like mine who, when she failed to institute a food-for-lipstick barter programme in Amman similar to the one established with Umm Samir in Jerusalem, fed her four kids and husband out-of-the-can green peas and Uncle Ben's rice, it is no wonder that I developed a fetish for gourmet food and gourmet friends. Not only did she hardly cook anything else, but Mama managed to build a whole myth, which sadly I believed for the longest time, that preparing good rice is one of the most difficult tasks in gourmet cooking. And since she did that, day in and day out, she had qualified herself as an outstanding cook.

May God rest her soul, but what a gastronomic tragedy it all was!

Since I was enjoying the delicious truffle pasta, I saw no point in thinking further about my mother's tasteless cooking. And since I can never keep quiet for long, I asked Elie if he was ready for his presentation on Darwish in less than half an hour. Elie responded with a smile that spread from ear to ear and across his full cheeks that were flushed almost to the same tint as the red wine he was still sipping. He gave me a mischievous look through his thick round glasses, then giggled and answered, 'Suad, do you know the Arabic expression *"Jai u jaieb 'edet il naseb ma'uh"*?' He arrived with his bluffing tool-kit. Elie meant that he had made people believe that he had become an expert on Mahmoud Darwish – although actually Elie had done a translation from Arabic to French that many experts consider the very best translation ever made of Darwish's poetry in any language.

Even though I must have heard this expression numerous times before, it was only then that I realised how humorous and original it was. I imagined an enormous man, as huge as Elie himself, carrying a gigantic box, but unlike Pandora's box with all the evils of the world, Elie's bluffing-box contained a stock of fine words, well-turned phrases, striking images, and scraps of poetry and elegant prose. With these he would soon captivate his audience, the way his reference to the bluffing-box had captivated me.

Although I was sitting next to Elie, I somehow missed the beginning of another story he had started telling Jamil, who was seated at the other end of the table.

'*Mais bien sûr*, yes, they sold him the air.'

'What! They sold him the air, the sky, the space above your own house!' Jamil almost choked on his *cinghiale*.

'Yes, they claim that the air above my house is not mine but theirs, so they gave the "building air rights", i.e. the right to construct a high-rise building on top of my two-storey house, to a businessman from Tel Aviv.'

Totally puzzled, I had to interrupt Elie.

'Wait, wait, wait! Elie, I'm truly sorry but I missed the beginning of your story. Who is selling what?' I demanded.

'I'm talking about my house in Haifa. You know I own a house in Haifa, don't you?' Elie asked in the same animated manner he had used when discussing cheese and wine.

'Of course, I know you own a house in Haifa.'

Prolific writer though he is, I, like many others, have read, heard about, or seen all that Elie has written throughout his life. So I was aware that his family comes from Haifa and that in 1948, when Elie was two and a half, his family had fled to Lebanon and he had grown up in Beirut. In the early 1970s he went to study in France and then returned to Beirut only to leave it again right after the Israeli invasion of Lebanon in 1982. He had been living permanently in Paris since then. But this was the very first time I had heard him talk about his house in Haifa.

I was gratified to hear Elie use the personal pronouns 'I' and 'my'. The Israelis think that over time, as the Palestinian Nakba generation disappears, their grabbing of Arab properties will become easier, or be accomplished de facto.

Time makes Palestinians forget. Time makes Jews remember.

'Yes, what about your house in Haifa?' I was very curious to know.

Elie took a Montblanc pen out of his pocket and started sketching a diagram of his house on my yellow paper placemat. I pushed my truffle plate aside to make room for his house in Haifa.

'My house is in al Hadar, il Carmel, so it is on a very steep slope.' In Picasso-like freehand, Elie drew two parallel lines and connected them with a curved arrow indicating a steep slope. Actually the word *hadar* is probably Hebrew for the

163

Arabic *munhadar*, meaning the steep slope. But, like everything else, they have eaten the *mun*.

'Yes, I know it's very steep,' I said to assure Elie that I was listening attentively to him. I was now also following his words as an architect.

'You see, the Israeli Custodian of Palestinian Absentee Property had forbidden the Arab tenants who live in my house from making any repairs to the building over the years.' I knew this, and I also knew that the prohibition against maintaining Arab property applied to both Arab landlords and their tenants.

While Elie was absorbed in drawing an elongated cube that represented his house, I relished the fact that the users, tenants and occupants – all those benefiting from Elie's house in Haifa – were Arabs and not, as was often the case, Israelis. 'Thank God that the people living in your house are Palestinians.'

'Yes, they're Palestinians from the village of Fassoutah,' Elie responded, while still concentrating on the rough sketch of his house in Haifa. He added a three-arched gallery to the lower level of the cube, a large rectangular opening indicating a terrace on the second floor, and two small windows on either side. Across the right side of the cube he drew two parallel inclined lines indicating a staircase connecting the two floors.

While still sketching Elie resumed his story. 'As a result of the Israeli policy, the tenants could not repair the staircase leading to the house and so the stairs collapsed. This meant that the tenants could no longer get to the second floor from the garden. They now reach it from the upper road.'

Here Elie added two straight arrows indicating the new entrance: a bridge connecting the house with the upper road.

I was a bit confused as to how the residents managed to get into the house from the back street, but I did not allow my obsession with technical details to distract Elie or me from the story.

'One day Muntaser, my tenant, called me from Haifa to tell me that he had recently received a letter from the Israeli Custodian of Absentee Property informing him that they had sold the air, the air rights, the air space above my house, to a businessman from Tel Aviv who had plans to build a high-rise on top of my two-storey house.' Elie stopped, took a deep breath, several sips of wine, followed by his usual '*Bien sûr!*' and a big smile.

I do not know what it is about Palestinians that makes them smile or even laugh at a time when they should be crying.

At this point Elie vertically extended the dimensions of his cubic house, indicating the future high-rise planned by the businessman from Tel Aviv. He then raised his head waiting for our feedback.

'*Veramente fanculo*,' said Anna. See how expressive Italian can be!

Jamil went into a fit of laughter, which was infectious.

'Are you sure that the man from Tel Aviv is a businessman and not an astronaut?' A typical Jamil comment.

'*Bien sûr . . . bien sûr*, an Israeli businessman from Tel Aviv,' Elie confirmed.

The animated discussion fell into a deep silence, which was soon broken by Piera's question, 'Suad, who normally owns or has the air space above a building?'

I must admit I was extremely challenged by her question. 'Hmm, well . . . let's see . . . it all depends . . . theoretically it all depends on the building regulations of the Municipality of

Haifa. If the building law allows four floors then you, Elie, have the right to add another two floors; if the law allows for seven or eight floors then again you have the right to build that many floors. If your house was in Manhattan, then you would have the right to build up to a hundred or a hundred and twenty floors. It all depends on the zoning and building regulations of the Haifa Municipality.'

I was responding as if the Israelis were normal people in a normal country.

Oh God, I thought, Israeli actions on the ground are challenging enough, but now we have to deal with their absurdities in the skies too! My mind was already occupied trying to figure out the ingenuity of suspending that bloody high-rise building from the skies without touching the ground.

I was so challenged by all this that I was about to admit to Elie and the others that, as an architecture student, I had failed all structural courses, but thank God Jamil saved me from that embarrassment.

'Wait until they claim underground rights and start building parking garages or tunnels below your property, then your two-floor house will become a falafel sandwiched between their two claimed rights to heaven and hell,' Jamil said.

'Air rights might reasonably apply when it comes to security or flight zones, not when it comes to building,' I said, feeling the heavy weight of responsibility for making sense of Israeli ingenuity.

'Well, with Israel there are always original ideas when it comes to stripping Palestinians of their rights, whether on the ground, below ground, in the sea or, as now, in the air,' said Jamil.

Obsessively trying to figure out how the structure of that

damn high-rise would drop from the sky, I offered a hesitant thought: 'But some structural elements of the new building will have to touch your land, unless they find a way to drop it from the air.'

'Drop it from where?' asked Elie.

'From the sky.'

'From God's seventh heaven.'

'*Min 'ind Rabna*, from on high.'

'Or from hell?'

I know for a fact that once we start being too dependent and demanding of God it means we have despaired.

And obviously we have lost hope.

Elie looked at his watch, got up and left hurriedly, leaving us all hanging in the air.

As I walked the rainy streets of Bellinzona I wondered whether the heaviness I felt in my head was caused by the *vino rosso corposo*?

Or by the Custodian of Absentee Property?

Or the result of contemplating the genius of the business-man from Tel Aviv?

As I stepped into the Teatro Sociale I saw Elie under the orange stage lights. I took my seat, closed my eyes and listened to Elie's *corposo* voice:

'On this land there is something worth living for. Mahmoud Darwish.'

Part Five

Homage to My Mother-in-Law
1911–2005

15.

That Very Moment

S HE HAD NEVER NARRATED this particular story before.
I had never asked. But this time I did.

Umm Salim must have been extremely surprised to hear
me insist that she tell me, in detail, her 1948 story. I wanted
to know everything about that day and that very moment
when she, her husband, Edmon, and their two-year-old son,
Salim, fled from their home in Jaffa.

My out-of-the-blue request perplexed my mother-in-law
and made her a bit distrustful. She must have recalled the
boredom on mine and Salim's face whenever she told and
retold stories about her childhood and youthful years in Jaffa.
'In Jaffa we went to the sea every weekend. In Jaffa we had
huge orange groves. In Jaffa we cooked this way. In Jaffa we
often went shopping in Tel Aviv. *Ihna ahel Yafa*. In Jaffa
people did it this way . . . and in Jaffa we did it that way . . .'
and so on and so forth.

If you weren't from Jaffa, and many were not, you would
certainly feel you had missed out on paradise, and had no
place amongst the fortunate Jaffans. And many did.

I had realised only lately that in spite of the many stories she
repeated over and over, my mother-in-law never mentioned
anything about that day.

Of the day she left home and was never allowed back.

She never said anything.

And I never asked.

But today was the very first time I was eager to have her tell her story and listen very carefully to every word she said. I wanted to make sure I would remember all that she had to tell me. I even recorded it.

It was the loss of my own mother two months earlier in February 2005 that made me realise the need to listen carefully to my ninety-four-year-old mother-in-law. I was trying to compensate for the loss of my mother, and with her, the loss of the minute details of how the Jewish forces dragged my father's family, my aunt and uncle, out of their home in Jaffa, and how the intense shooting and the occupation of their house forced my parents to leave their home in Jerusalem.

What amazes me most is that we, as a people, have shared our collective story of being thrown out of our homeland, Palestine, with each other and with many others – actually we have bored the world with this collective story – but somehow the individual Palestinian shies away, or perhaps is too afraid, to share the very personal story of being thrown out of her or his home, living room, or bedroom. These personal stories are seldom told, not even to our own children, perhaps not even to ourselves.

I guess the wound remains open.

Yet even though Umm Salim lived in Ramallah for fifty-five years, I rarely heard her tell a story about her life in Ramallah or use the expression 'we in Ramallah', the town where she lived for over half a century; the town where she died at the age of ninety-four.

Though it was not her wish, Umm Salim was buried in Ramallah.

Jaffa in the 1940s

Having been married to Umm Salim's only son for the last twenty-one years, I knew by now that she came from a big family. She had six brothers and one sister: 'Me and Claire were treated like queens, particularly me. I was difficult and . . .'

'Still are,' I said jokingly. Or perhaps not so jokingly.

'I was difficult and fussy when it came to food,' she continued.

'Only when it came to food!' I was taking advantage of the situation, but Umm Salim ignored my comments and carried on.

'My mother had two helpers, but she still had eight spoilt children and a very demanding husband. Despite that, she managed to pamper each and every one of us: from little Qaisar who once fell down the well, got diabetes as a result and died very young, to Najib, the eldest and most difficult. Najib was so fussy about his clothes, I can't tell you.'

And of course, I can't tell you how many times Umm Salim had told me the same story over and over again. Not only that, but every time she mentioned her youngest brother, Qaisar, she would add the refrain: poor thing he once fell down the well, became diabetic and died very young.

'In spite of everything, we were all extremely well-disciplined: no matter what, we all had to sit around the big dining table for the three meals of the day. I do not remember one time when we did not eat together: no one was allowed to come home late for lunch or dinner; they would not be fed if they did.'

'Umm Salim . . . this all sounds very familiar!' Again she ignored me.

'Poor Mama, she would prepare a different dish for each one of us: Najib did not eat meat, Claire did not like chicken,

I couldn't stand spinach, Elias couldn't stand the smell of cabbage or cauliflower, Baba did not eat liver while Toni loved it, Qaisar (poor thing he once . . .) was vegetarian, and so on and so on.

'Out of respect, all of us, except Mama, had to be seated at the table before Baba arrived exhausted from work. As soon as Mama heard his footsteps on the stairs she would run to open the door, welcome him, then help him take off his jacket or coat and hang it up for him. Mother would only sit after Baba had washed his face and hands and sat down at the head of the table.

'"Shhh, your father is tired, keep quiet." We had to be quiet as long as Baba was at home, and remain completely silent for the duration of his two-hour siesta, which he took religiously every single afternoon of his life.

'However, I must say that the biggest shock of my life was when my schoolteacher inquired about my father's job. I had no clue. I came running home and asked Mama, "What does Baba do for a living?" She looked me in the face and said with all seriousness, "Your Baba is a landlord," and when I asked what that entailed she said, "He collects the rents at the end of every month or at the end of every year." Expecting my teacher to inquire further, I asked Mama, "And what does Baba do when he's not collecting rent once a month or once a year?" She answered, "He spends the rest of his time in the coffee shop playing cards or backgammon with other landlords."

'Poor Mama, there she was, killing herself taking care of a family of ten while Baba was sitting in the coffee shop . . . collecting rent from three shops and one house . . . that must have been truly hard work!'

Umm Salim broke into hearty laughter at this point.

'From that day on I never hushed for Baba or any other man in my whole life.'

To me that was pretty obvious.

'Our Cirque Sportif club' – this said in her French accent – 'in Jaffa was highly exclusive. It was reserved for *il Catolic* only. Not even Orthodox Christians were allowed in (not to mention Muslims). Remember Signore Alonzo?' she posed the question then carried on, 'He was in charge of our club!' Not wanting to spoil my mother-in-law's romanticised memories of Jaffa, I kept the response to myself. Of course I remembered Signore Alonzo. He was the one who, in 1981, became very reluctant to help me locate my father's house in the Manshiyeh neighbourhood of Jaffa the minute he realised that I was not a Christian.

'Down, down there . . .' he had said in a dismissive tone and an even more dismissive hand gesture in reference to the poorer Manshieh neighbourhood, which was predominantly Muslim. If Alonzo was in charge of the Cirque Sportive, of course no Muslim ever made it to the club.

It was such sectarian and class-conscious comments that made her secular leftist son, Salim, feel so embarrassed by what his mother said. He would often change the subject or simply roll his eyes and walk out of the room.

'I never wanted to marry. I never liked men. Actually, I was never attracted to men,' Umm Salim said with a straight face. I smiled and kept quiet.

'Before Edmon and I were married, we went on a date to visit my brother Elias in Haifa. On the way there, all of a sudden Edmon grabbed me tightly and gave me a kiss.'

Hmm . . . a kiss, I thought to myself, but before I had a

chance to visualise or even romanticise about that very first kiss, Umm Salim went on, 'And in return, he got a big slap on his face. "Wow," I said, "Who gave you permission to kiss me?" Edmon just smiled.'

My mother-in-law burst out laughing when she recalled this slap-for-a-kiss exchange more than sixty years later.

But I must say that I was not at all surprised by this chaste episode. Ever since I had known her, my mother-in-law had never liked being kissed by anyone. I dare say not even by her own son. 'Yech, I can't stand it when people kiss me, I don't know why they do that! Aren't they afraid of microbes?' she would say, rubbing the kiss off her cheek if, for one reason or another, she could not prevent that sudden Mediterranean exchange of two or three kisses in a row.

'Suad dear, make sure you have two separate beds, yech. I can't stand it when someone breathes in my face.' That was the very first bit of advice my mother-in-law gave me when her adorable son and I were getting married.

And then she wondered why we never had children. 'Every summer all the girls and boys of our Cirque Sportive would go swimming in the sea. Often we got on a *hasakeh*, a kind of heavy, keeled surf board. A boy and a girl sat on each board; we girls sat in front while the boys sat behind with the double oars.

'Once we were in the middle of the sea when the boy behind me came up close, grabbed me and then circled my waist with his hands. I got so disgusted and panicky that I threatened to drown myself! This threw him into a panic and he instantly removed his hands.'

'No slapping the face this time,' I jested, and thought, poor

176

boy. Then I remembered how Salim often referred to his father: *Miskeen Baba*. Poor Baba. When I asked her whether she remembered the boy's name she said, 'No, why would I?' then continued, 'I never liked it when boys touched me. It disgusted me. I was very strict.'

'I bet not all the girls were as strict as you were, Umm Salim!' I teased. She instantly replied, 'Nooo, no, of course not. There were these two naughty girls who would often squeeze Edmon between them until he blushed and turned all red . . . poor thing, he was extremely shy.'

With a mother-in-law who didn't like boys to touch her and a shrinking violet for a husband, I always wondered how my own husband, Salim, made it into this world.

It was not the first time that I'd heard my mother-in-law tell this story, of course. Like most of her Jaffa tales, she repeated it again and again whenever she had an ear willing to listen, which was rarely mine and hardly ever Salim's.

The baker who fled town
14 May 1948

She had never narrated this particular story before.

I had never asked. But this time I did.

'It wasn't until that early morning when Milaneh, our housemaid, came back with the unbaked dough that I realised it was no longer possible for us to stay in our home,' said Umm Salim.

'"The baker fled town last night," announced Milaneh.'

Knowing how well my mother-in-law cooked and baked, I was not entirely convinced that she would flee her house, her beloved town and her own country because the baker had left. She must have seen the disbelief on my face, so she tried to give a more convincing account.

'Well, the day before our house had been hit badly from that side,' she raised her head and pointed, with stretched arm and upper body, to the ceiling of her Ramallah house. 'I mean from the direction of Tel Aviv, from where all the shooting was coming. There was also no water, no telephone lines, and perhaps no electricity; I can't really remember whether we had electricity at that point or not. All I recall is that we painted all the glass in our windows navy blue during the 1948 war.'

She paused for a second and then continued. 'Edmon was adamant not to leave home. We were planning to stay put even though most members of both our families had already left for Beirut weeks earlier. As you know, our families used to go to Mount Lebanon every summer but that year, because of the war, they had gone a month or two earlier, except for my brother Fu'ad, who stayed behind to look after my parents' house and Baba's businesses, and Abdallah, Edmon's brother, who also stayed behind with his wife, Julia, to take care of their house. As you know, Suad, many houses were broken into and robbed.'

Having been born a few years after the war I knew nothing, of course, but kept quiet.

'Edmon was the *inspecteur*' – I could not but smile as her French accent reminded me of Inspecteur Clouseau – 'of Socony-Vacuum which later became Mobil Oil. Therefore he and I knew well that the rumours about a petrol shortage, which would soon make it impossible to escape the heavily bombarded city, were actually true. Being in charge of all Socony-Vacuum employees as well as their cars, Edmon had given strict instructions to all to stay put. So how could we leave them behind?' Umm Salim asked in a responsible voice, some fifty-seven years later.

Until the day she died, 30 October 2005, Umm Salim received a monthly pension from Mobil Oil, now Exxon Mobil. 'That week all of Jaffa, but mostly our neighbourhood, al Ajami, was badly hit by intensified shelling from Tel Aviv. The day before we left, all the Socony-Vacuum employees who worked under Edmon came to inform him that they had made up their minds. The situation had become unbearably dangerous so they and their families were leaving town. They also admitted to their boss that, behind his back, they had been storing gallons and gallons of petrol in order to drive themselves and their families to Beirut. They were going to hand in the cars to the Socony-Vacuum main offices in Beirut.'

Realising the limits of his authority over the destinies of his employees and their terrified families, Edmon then asked them for a few gallons of petrol for his own car.

At the break of dawn

'It was very early in the morning when we left. Milaneh made the coffee, got Salim dressed, and off we went to Beirut via Ramallah with our suitcases. Edmon, Salim and I. Milaneh stayed behind.'

End of story.

She had never narrated this particular story before.

I had never asked. But this time I did.

Like many historic moments, that night acquired significance retrospectively, when they realised they would not be allowed to go back home.

She looked at me, flashed me a subtle smile, stared straight ahead, then began talking. 'All I remember about that night before we left is that it was long and humid, with a deadly silence broken only by erratic shooting. Edmon and I alternated tossing in bed.'

'And then?'

'At the break of dawn Milaneh knocked at our bedroom door. Sensing that we had not slept that night, she hurried straightaway to the kitchen, made us coffee, a large pot of coffee and some sandwiches, and then went to get Salim ready. I got out of bed and slipped into the clothes I had put out the night before. Without uttering a word, Edmon did the same.'

Knowing well how much time my perfectly matched, elegant mother-in-law needed to get herself ready, it was not easy for me to visualise the slipping-into-her-clothes scene. And I could not help but be frivolous and think of those stale-bread sandwiches. Not realising that she would not set foot in her home ever again, I am sure slipping into her clothes and eating sandwiches made with stale bread were the real Nakba for my fussy, gourmet mother-in-law.

'Being anxious about leaving, neither of us was up to breakfast. Without sitting down we each took a few quick sips of coffee, placed our half-full cups on the living room table and hurriedly left the room. While I carefully carried Salim down the two flights of stairs, Edmon and Milaneh brought down the heavy suitcases. With Milaneh's help, Edmon loaded the suitcases in the trunk, then cautiously and swiftly slipped into the driver's seat. I settled down in the passenger seat next to Edmon, with a cranky Salim on my lap.'

I was about to beg my mother-in-law to sit in the back seat

with my two-year-old husband, but since they were both safe and sound now, she at the age of ninety-four and he at sixty, it seemed an utterly unnecessary piece of cautionary advice.

'We said goodbye to Milaneh, who promised to take care of the house. We had boarded up the windows and doors with thick wooden planks the day before.'

Umm Salim must have noticed me looking unhappy at the thought of leaving Milaneh behind in an empty house in a deserted city.

'Milaneh was to leave the next day on a boat which would bring her and her family to Beirut. And since there was a shortage of boats as thousands of people had waited for days on end on the shores of Jaffa in order to be picked up, I asked my cousin Habib Ghandur, whose family owned a boat company, to hurry up and bring more boats.'

I must say that Umm Salim did not seem to be bothered by leaving her maid behind. To avoid the guilty or innocent question I asked, 'Umm Salim, what did you take with you when you left home?'

'Not much, just summer clothes. At the time we didn't realise that this would be it. If I had known I would have carried a wedding present: a silver make-up set given to me by my women friends. It was truly beautiful.' There was a long pause before Umm Salim continued. 'Actually all the furniture in our house was brand new and beautiful.'

A longer pause.

'Since the government had taken every vacant house for its own employees, there was a severe shortage of houses. And since I adamantly refused to live with my in-laws . . .'

Without meaning to, the words escaped my mouth, 'Lucky in-laws.'

But Umm Salim was preoccupied with her own story. 'Edmon and I were engaged for three long years during which we carefully selected every single item and stacked it in a room at my in-laws', until one day we heard of an unoccupied house, and in agreement with its owners, we sneaked in late at night and arranged the furniture in all the rooms.

'As long as I live I shall never forget that night. The house looked fabulous the next day: I tell you, the dining table was very special. To this day I haven't seen anything like it. It had three curves at each end, and when extended it was just beautiful. We had bought it from a furniture shop in Tel Aviv, but it had been brought by the Mascob from Russia.'

At this point I could just see Umm Salim going from one room to another in her house in Jaffa, admiring her furniture. After a long pause she looked at the low coffee table on which we had placed our coffee cups.

'The coffee table was just gorgeous. Most coffee tables back then had square and bulky legs, but this one had very thin and elegant ones, delicately curved. Suad, let me show you what I mean.' Umm Salim stood up, took me by the hand and led me to the guest room.

'See how beautiful and thin her legs are?' (The word 'table' happens to be feminine in Arabic.) 'Have you ever seen anything like this?' she was gazing at the coffee table in the middle of the room.

My mother-in-law's sensual description of the coffee table legs sounded more like a description of a gorgeous female lover she had left behind in Jaffa. Her not liking boys touching her, and now these erotic descriptions of a (feminine) table made me suspect my mother-in-law had lesbian tendencies.

'Did you end up bringing her, I mean the table, with you to Ramallah, Umm Salim?'

'No, no . . . but I had it made again by the same carpenter who had also fled Jaffa for Beirut.'

I had tears in my eyes. I felt so bad that in all these years I had never noticed either the coffee table or its shapely, slender legs.

'Every single carpenter in Ramallah has come to see her elegant and beautifully curved legs,' she added as she walked back to the glazed veranda of her Ramallah house.

I was gazing out of her window at Arafat's mausoleum when she spoke again. 'I think Salim was about two and a half when we left Jaffa. He was born 2 August 1945. I got pregnant right away, I think the night we got married.'

I could not help but think that she wanted to get it over with as quickly as possible. 'And I bet that was about the only time you allowed Abu Salim, Edmon, to touch you.'

She cracked up laughing. '*Ta'riban*, just about.'

'No wonder you had only one child, but that was pretty efficient.' I had a feeling that my mother-in-law liked talking about lost sex more than a lost house or a lost country.

'Mother, were you aware then that Salim was born in the same year, the same month, even the same day as the bombing of Hiroshima?' I interrupted.

'Hiroshima? Oh, yes,' she replied indifferently.

She had never narrated this particular story before and I had never asked. But this time I insisted she tell me in detail: 'And then?'

'Soon we were near Edmon's brother's house . . . hmm . . . what was his name? You see, I forget these days. Oh yes, Abdallah. On the way to Abdallah's house we saw many deserted cars and trucks loaded with people's belongings and furniture. Some had been shelled but others were abandoned because they had run out of petrol. People were carrying their blankets and belongings and walking towards the seashore; many slept there for days on end. When we got to Abdallah's house to tell him that we were leaving, to say goodbye, he, his wife, Julia, and his son, Elias, were in total panic.

'"Oh, no . . . we're not staying behind all by ourselves, the whole family has already left . . . please wait . . . wait, we're coming with you," Abdallah begged.

'"But we don't have a place for you in the car, we've got a few gallons of petrol in the back seat," I said.

'"Don't worry, Marie. Julia, Elias and I will put the petrol on our laps," Abdallah insisted.

'"But that is dangerous and stupid!" I screamed back at him.

'"Certainly not as dangerous as staying behind all alone. You saw how much shooting and shelling there's been from Tel Aviv in the last few days." Both Elias and Julia were hurriedly collecting a few personal belongings as Abdallah argued with me. Poor Edmon, he kept quiet. Well, ultimately I gave in,' said Umm Salim.

'Eventually we drove away with an overcrowded car: Salim in my lap, a gallon of petrol in Abdallah's lap, another in Julia's, and a third in seventeen-year-old Elias'.'

At that point, I was getting more interested in family gossip. 'Come on, Umm Salim, it had nothing to do with having or not having room in your car. Admit it, you never liked Julia or Abdallah.' I was purposely abusing my insider information to instigate more vicious family gossip, and I got it.

'Actually, I didn't mind Julia, she was naïve and stupid. It

184

was Abdallah's guts I couldn't stand. He was such a Don Juan. Julia was filthy rich. Her family had so much gold they hoarded it in jars. Abdallah spent all her money travelling abroad, to Lebanon and Europe, having a good time all by himself he claimed, while flirting with all sorts of women. Then, as if she were a little girl, he would bring his wife a pretty hat with a ribbon. She would proudly go around town wearing it and bragging about her husband's love and the silly presents he gave her. Aaah, I never liked the way he treated his wife.'

At moments like these, I suspected that my mother-in-law was an earlier Simone de Beauvoir of the Arab world with no first or second sex.

'And . . .?' I insisted.

'A few weeks later I went to check on Milaneh. She was quarantined at the port in Beirut. "Madame, stay away from me, don't come any closer," she said when I greeted her from a distance.'

Knowing my mother-in-law's hypochondria I was not worried about her getting any closer to Milaneh. Actually I was surprised she went to the Quarantine Bay in the first place, but household help was essential for my mother-in-law.

'"We've been contaminated by microbes. We must've picked up some disease on the overcrowded boat that carried us from Jaffa to Beirut. The Lebanese have decided to keep us in quarantine for forty days."'

After a short pause Umm Salim continued. 'During that same visit, Milaneh gave me the bad news that our house was robbed the very day we left it. It seems that all the effort we put into nailing wooden planks on all the windows had been useless.'

I was profoundly disturbed by the robbery in my in-laws' house, even though it had happened so many decades ago. It made me so angry, it felt as if it were happening today.

Pain and loss have no logic.

'Come, Suad, let me show you the one thing I still have from our house in Jaffa.'

Umm Salim stood up, gripping my arm tightly. I followed. She walked into the corridor leading to her bedroom, paused, then pointed at a gilded icon hanging on the wall.

'You see this *iqouneh*, Suad?' she asked excitedly.

'Yes,' I replied, staring at Christ's gilded face.

Oh, God. I don't believe this icon has been hanging on this wall for so many years and I never noticed how beautiful it was. Shame on you, Suad. Like typical Russian or Greek icons painted on wood, this one had the shape of a book: yes, a thirty by twenty centimetre metal book, five centimetres thick.

The icon consisted of a florally-decorated gilded sheet in the middle of which were three cuts or openings: one around Christ's head and long hair, another around his left palm in which he held an open bible, and a third around his right hand. The movement of his fingers suggested a cross.

The brown colouring of Christ's head and his two hands contrasted nicely with the gilded background. The halo around the head, the script in the Bible and the hems of the wide robe draped over him were all decorated in white, again contrasting beautifully with the gold. I was totally absorbed in the delicate decorations of the halo around Christ's head when I heard Umm Salim speak again.

'This is an extremely valuable *iqouneh*, Suad. It's made of gilded metal and was given to us as a present by an uncle of

186

Edmon's who lived in Jerusalem, I can't remember his name now.'

'But Mother, I thought you didn't take any valuables with you when you left home!'

'True, I didn't. But a year or two later a Russian nun who claimed to have bought it in Jaffa brought it to me in Beirut, or perhaps in Ramallah. I was happy to re-acquire it. I paid her what she asked for, all the money we had then. I think it was around one hundred and fifty dinars.'

Having paid in dinars made me suspect that the Russian nun would have brought it to Umm Salim after she, Edmon and Salim came to live in Ramallah in 1951.

Umm Salim also learnt that her beloved dining table, the Persian carpets given to her by her brother Najib, and other items of her furniture were up for sale as well.

'But at that point we didn't have the money to buy back the rest of our stolen furniture.'

Jaffa / Tel Aviv

It must have been in the mid-1990s.

Shumuel and I were sitting in the back seat chatting in the most polite and over-friendly tones – the fake manner often used by Palestinians and Israelis when talking to one another in an attempt to hide the exasperation they feel towards each other.

That late evening I was returning to Jerusalem from Tel Aviv where I had participated in a seminar on the prospects of peace between Palestinians and Israelis.

At that time there was still hope.

Shumuel, who sat right next to me, was a rather friendly

middle-aged Israeli politician who had apparently also taken part in another seminar at the same conference.

In the same over-friendly tone Shumuel told me that he was at one time a high-ranking Mossad agent. Oh my God, Shumuel Toledano, I gasped, and almost fainted. I trembled to my very core. Shumuel must have sensed it from my glazed eyes, expressionless face and stiffening body.

But no.

He, in exactly the same friendly tone, continued to share with me, in Arabic, our common history, once he knew we were originally from Jaffa.

'Right after the battle of Jaffa ended in May 1948 the town was totally deserted. Many Palestinians had left their homes. I remember vividly how I, together with other Jewish soldiers, entered one of the Arab houses in al Ajami. On the coffee table in the middle of the living room was a pot of coffee, still warm, that someone must have made that very morning but had to leave behind in a hurry . . .'

After a long pause he continued, 'You know, Suad, as long as I live I shall never forget that moment.'

Nor will I.

Through my tightly clenched teeth I tried to take a deep breath to stop the tears from brimming over in my eyes. Immediately, I felt a sourness in my throat.

Although I managed not to cry that afternoon, my tears and my voice always fail me whenever I try to tell that story.

At Umm Salim's house in Ramallah, on the veranda, she and I drank our cups of coffee as we gazed out the window into the horizon where that other pot of coffee had been left behind.

The Never-Ending Chapter

My country: As close to me as my prison.

Mahmoud Darwish

Would You Ever Let Go of Me?

Would you ever let go of me
For a lifetime
For a year
A month
An hour
A minute
Even a second?

No

If ever
If ever we get an apology
If ever we get compensation for our losses
It would not be about a lost country
It would not be about a lost field
Or an orange grove
Or a lost home

No

It would not be about the hundreds of bulldozed villages
Or the scattering of a whole nation
The shattering of a whole society
It would not be about losing a livelihood
A stolen piano, a Persian carpet or a first baby photo
    album
And it would not be about someone's personal library
An abandoned Arab horse or a Cypriot donkey
Nor a Persian cat nor even Shasa, the monkey that my
    mother gave me a few days before the war

No

And it would not be about the blossoming almond trees
    and the red flowering pomegranates that were not
    picked tenderly in the spring of 1948 nor the
    following summer
And it would not be about firing at the farmers who
    returned to harvest the fields they had left behind
Nor would it be about the many deserted budding roses
Or a bride's wardrobe and her many cherished wedding
    gifts
Or a child or an old woman who was forgotten, left
    behind in the chaos

No

It would not be about concealing a crime or falsifying
    history

It would not be about blaming the victim
It would not be about dehumanisation and stereotyping
It would not be about making new 'wandering Jews' out
    of us
It would not be about reversing roles and images

No

If at all
It will only be about an obsession
Yes, an obsession

My dreams are all about you
And my nightmares are all because of you
My happiness is related to you
And my sadness comes from you
My expectations are all concerning you
And my disappointments pile up beside you

Yes

And if I run away, I run away from you
And if I come back, I come back to you
If I love someone, it is because of what they think of you
And if I hate someone, it is because of what they say
    about you

Yes

And it is because of you:
Nothing in my life is normal

Nothing in my life is neutral
Nothing is mundane
Or even insignificant

And how very exhausting it is

How I desire one ordinary day when you do not haunt
   me
How I long for a pleasant evening where you are not
   invited
How I yearn to forget you
How I wish for amnesia or a stroke that
Will neatly remove every trace of you: Thoughts,
   memories, emotions
Gone forever
I heard them moan for you before I was born
And I heard them moan for you after I was born and
   ever after
Their bedtime stories are about you
And their daydreaming is also about you
I've seen them cry, laugh, praise and curse

You, you, and only YOU
I had to learn everything about you
I had to imagine you from across a border
Miss you
Love you
Defend you
Cry for you
Write about you
Talk about you

And, in imperative form, love you

And how very exhausting it is

Above all I have to keep my sanity with all the brutality
    around you
Every hour every minute and every second
If ever I do come to terms with what has happened to
    you I must banish that part of my brain
That cherishes reason, logic and justice

Palestine

Will you ever set us free?

Glossary

Absentee landlords: In the context of this book this term refers to the 850,000 Palestinians who were thrown out of their homeland and homes never to be allowed access to the properties (land, homes, buildings as well as mobile properties) left behind when they became refugees in 1948.

Arnona: Israel property tax.

Asfourah: Asfourah in Arabic literally means 'bird', and in this context, an informer. It is a common practice in Israeli prisons to extract information before interrogations or court trials by planting informers amongst detainees.

George Bisharat: A Palestinian–American professor of law and author of an article about visiting his own house: 'Talbiyah Days: At Villa Harun al-Rashid in Jerusalem' in *Jerusalem Quarterly* 30: Vol. 8, No 2. Spring 2007, pp. 88–98.

Diplomatic missions: Of all the pre-1948 diplomatic missions in Jerusalem, fourteen continue to function in both parts of the divided city. After the creation of Israel in 1948, Tel Aviv was declared its capital and new embassies opened there. After 1994 and the creation of the Palestinian National Authority, new missions opened in Ramallah.

East and West Jerusalem: The city is called Jerusalem, however in 1947 when the UN Security Council approved the creation of the state of Israel, Jerusalem was given a *corpus-separatum* status. As a result of the 1948 partition, the city was divided into West and East. Hence the new expressions, West and East, Jewish and Arab Jerusalem.

Jerusalem syndrome: This term and the term 'the crazed of Jerusalem' refer to the noticeably numerous psychologically distressed people walking the streets of Jerusalem.

Mamillah Cemetery: A Muslim cemetery located in West Jerusalem. In July 2011, the Israeli Ministry of Interior gave official approval for the construction of a Museum of Tolerance on the cemetery site, with work to start immediately. Two weeks later, Palestinian community leaders asked the UN and UNESCO to intervene to stop the desecration of the cemetery, which is well over a thousand years old. The Center for Constitutional Rights, a US non-profit organisation, and the Protection of the Mamillah Cemetery Campaign continue to advocate for the preservation of this historic and sacred site.

Mount Scopus: In this context it refers to a part of the Hebrew University located on Mount Scopus in East Jerusalem. It constitutes an enclave that continued to be under Israeli control between 1948 and 1967.

Palestine Broadcasting Service: The Palestine Broadcasting Service was the second biggest in the region after Radio Cairo, and was established by British Mandate authorities in order to have a powerful media tool to influence the Arab public towards British policies in the region.

Harun al-Rashid: A ninth-century Abbasid Caliph in Baghdad known for his wise rule, great wealth, and interest in promoting cultural and intellectual growth.

Acknowledgements

Since I became a writer accidentally some ten years ago, I obviously never knew what writer's block was all about until it hit me in 2009 and kept me 'company' for two long years. And it only let go of me at the end of 2011 when *Golda* took command of me, and my writing.

And who in their right mind dares say no to Golda?

Born a *hakawati*, a storyteller, rather than a skilful writer, until writer's block hit me I almost always managed, rather easily, to allow the story within me to come out and scribble itself on a piece of paper or on the screen of my PC.

The writer's block meant, amongst many other things, an interruption of my so far two-year publishing cycle: *Sharon and My Mother-in-Law* (2003), *Se Questa E' Vita* (2005), *Neinte Sesso in Citta'* (2007), and *Murad Murad* (2009), hence the skipping of a book in 2011.

One thing I share with most, if not all, authors is egocentricity; I expected my readers and my publisher(s) to bombard me with emails asking: 'Where are you Suad? We are anxiously waiting for a new book from you.' But of course none of that happened and as a result I even got more depressed. But that also made me aware that the very best way to have a writer overcome her or his writing block is by ignoring the block but never the writer. And that is exactly what professional Alberto Rollo (from Feltrinelli) and Maria Nadotti did during those two years: they gave me the attention that I obviously needed and delicately expressed their love and attention, without ever coming close to the sensitive question that all writers under block fear most . . . Thank you dear Alberto, thank you dear Maria and thank you Giovanna Silvia for always being there. Needless to say that Feltrinelli long ago acquired the status of a family for me.

First and foremost a very especial thanks goes to Alex Barmaki, my English editor. The impeccable English of Oxford gradu-ate Palestinian Alex, and his valuable remarks enriched the manuscript beyond recognition. Thank you, Alex, for reading and re-reading and re-re-reading the manuscript. Living with *Golda* for so many months was certainly beyond the call of duty. No writer loves his or her editor but I certainly do.

And before I forget I need to thank Salim Tamari. In spite of him being my husband, his comments (on my writing) have always been instrumental: thank you Salim for also putting up with my constant nagging especially during the nerve-breaking time waiting to hear from my publishers.

Diala Khasawnih, my niece, thank you for always expressing a desire to read my manuscripts. Thank you for your valuable comments whose weight became obvious when my publisher seconded them! I also thank my sisters Arwa and Anan who promptly replied to my numerous inquiries about our family's life in Jerusalem before I was born.

A special thanks goes to my closest three women friends for their support and inspirational words: to Marisa Savoia who encouraged me when the first draft of this book needed additional work: 'Suad imperfection make us grow'. Luisa Morgantini: 'Suad you sit-down and write and I do the cooking . . .' Oh how I wished it were the other way round. And Leila Chahid who once wrote me: 'Virginia Woolf, how is your writing going? Please give it attention: you are gifted and that is a blessing from God, particularly at our age!' Thank you, Leila, but I could have done without the age reference!

So as not to make this acknowledgement much longer I hereby thank: Nadia Saa' for suggesting the title of this book, to Lana Judeh, Hiafa Barmaki, Tania Tamari-Nasser, Noel Saleh, Zuleikha Aburisha, Alma Khasawnih, Saqer Abu Fakher, and Riwaq. A very special thanks goes to Mireille Safa, Beppe Chierici, and all the kind inhabitants of my little Italian village Pesciano/Umbria who provided me with all what a writer dreams of. Last but not least a special thanks goes to the Martin Luther King Public Library in Georgetown, Washington DC, where the bulk of this book was written in 2012.